Many Thanks!

## THE BOOK OF ASHES
## E S STEPHENS

First published in the UK 2021
Written by Elizabeth Stephens
Publisher and distribution: Ingram Spark
All rights reserved apart from any fair dealing for the purpose of study, research or review, as permitted under the Copyright, Designs and Patents Act 1988.
No part of this publication may be reproduced, stored in a retrieval system, or transmitted in any form, or by any means, electronical, chemical, mechanical, optical, photocopying, recording, or otherwise, without prior consent of the author.

www.esstephensauthor.co.uk

# Contents

| | |
|---|---|
| Foreword | 1 |
| Shadow in the Blood | 3 |
| Beneath the Skin | 31 |
| Drowned | 57 |
| Old Man Splinter | 75 |
| Superstition | 103 |
| Hero's Feast | 123 |
| Mud Men | 145 |
| Glossary of Names & Places | 158 |

# THE NORTHERN PLAINS

THE RIVER ANG OSEN

SHEVE

THE BOWL OF ARTUS

THE ARGON OCEAN

IMET

THE WILDLANDS OF KURTH

RIVER ACONITE

AGRELLON

THE FERN

NAETH ENNORE

THE BAY OF TEARS

THE GORGON'S HORN

N

THE URG

THE D E

SOUTHERN STRAIGHTS

NOGVOROD

# ANDS OF THE
# RAURHEGAR

MARIDA

NORTHERN STRAIGHTS

RANGE QUADRATA

SILVER FLOOD MARSHES

NIBACWKLIN

THE SILVER STONE RIVER

STILKINE

DARKTIDE

ORROWLIGHT

NIGHTMOTH VAYLE

FELNHAVEN

STOAMZEN

THE VAULT

ESARI

FORT VHEADARI

EVERFALL

FORT MELENAR  FORT KAORA  FORT DOVSHYRUN

THE FANGS OF EROTH

THE DUMA SEA

MOUTH OF MALINAX

THE DORO VOD CANAL

AR

KHERDROM

THE DUMAN CHANNEL

# FOREWORD

Welcome to *The Book of Ashes*, my first anthology of short fiction set in The Lands of the Draurhegar. If you have never read any of my previous titles and are picking up this book for the first time - fear not, you need no prior knowledge of the plot or mythos to any of those books. In fact, you could probably get along without any of the resources provided here. However, for the discerning readers among you, armed with the map and glossary, you have everything you need to feel fully immersed in this new world.

The Lands of the Draurhegar are the dark, untamed home where the monsters from childhood nightmares still roam. While the setting may indeed lie firmly in the fiction world, I ask you to suspend your disbelief for just a moment, for these creatures were once very real to our childish minds. This is not a book designed for children and though the setting of this land might appear fairytale-like in its medieval quality, it is a horrific parody of it.

In truth, this book is inspired by the great classics of Gothic literature. *Frankenstein, Dracula, The Phantom of the Opera, The Rise of Cthulhu*, and who could forget the many spooky tales from Edgar Allen Poe. These narratives have been tested by time and in turn have become timeless owing to their human outlook. They stand like mirrors, reflecting back at the reader the aspects of our humanity that we brush under the carpet: sexuality, ego, the other. All those wonderfully confusing psychological elements that make up what a human is, and some of those elements are far from flattering. It is upon these shoulders that Modern Gothic has been allowed to thrive. For reasons best left to the historians, we - the writers of this genre, have taken to our fictional worlds to re-explore the ugly issues and the things that are unpalatable save in fiction

War is largely considered one of if not 'the' most horrific thing, that humanity has brought to the world - we seem to thrive on it as do the fictional nations referred to in this book, none of which have been designed to represent any particular nation currently at large in the world today - perhaps ever. That is probably a good thing! War is something that at least in the 21st century, humans have become inured to. Indeed, there have been very few times where humanity has actually been at peace with itself. It is flung at us daily upon every news channel, blurred by our western focus. This is a book about a war. A war between two people that might not seem that dissimilar. Drau (who might be described as elf-like but are certainly not elves and would be extremely offended to be referred as such), are filled with their own superiority. They truly believe that they are at the very top of the food chain. Blood, or at least the purity of it, is of extreme importance and they have built a society specifically designed to exploit those beneath them with very few exceptions. Dwentari, bring the illumination of technology. An acceptance of all wrought beneath spinning cogs, forged metal, and the blood, sweat, and tears of its people. There are no 'good guys' but are there ever? In the end true horrors are enacted by those who hold the rod of power and are felt by those beneath its swing.

These are tales of the little man (or beast), the ones who lie so far down the list that they were easy to forget. Fantastical stories of very human feelings: a brother looking for a lost sister, a wife awaiting her husbands return, a soldier lost in strange lands, and more. Little pressures that might at once seem so insignificant, can suddenly grow into back-breaking efforts. Monsters that seemed fictional, can suddenly be real. A fear that once began to keep people safe from reasonable cause, can quickly turn into superstition.

No, this book is not for the faint of heart. So, tread carefully, keep the light on, the candle burning, and lock the door. The monsters are coming to have their say...

*G G Stephens*

*21st January 2021*

*Shadow in the Blood*

> "Some ghosts are so quiet you would hardly know they were there."
> —Bernie McGill, The Butterfly Cabinet

Eremis could hear the screams. A terrifying melody that drifted against the choir of the waves. It reached him even here, secluded as he had been in his cliff top cave. If he closed his eyes he could still taste the blood in his mouth and hear the drums. He remembered the foolish glow of hero's glory that had burned in his chest as he and a hundred militia had charged the Dwentari column. He blinked and the memory was banished.

Eremis was a towering giant of a man, tall even by Drau standards which tended naturally to the lithe and sinewy. He had been trained as a Watcher, a monster hunter of sought, in the council of Agrellon. He had claimed no titles, had taken no land, and claimed fealty to none save himself. He was a fearless hunter and for two years, he had hidden himself away here in this cave, sheltered from the concerns of the world, large and small. Two years was little to Drau and yet he felt old and frail as if a hundred had passed in their stead. Weak.

Angrily, he frayed the edge of his tattered cloak between his bony fingers. Hunger gnawed at him as it had done for days. Soon he would have to leave and scavenge whatever the sea had sought to leave him. He look at the half-light of the new day through the cave's entrance. Maybe tomorrow, or the day after.

*"Eremis, Warden of the Wild, wise counsel and guardian. Do you hear me?"*

It was her voice again. He pulled his legs into his chest and rocked slightly against the stone floor. Back and forth, back and forth.

*"Watcher, hear me. There is little time."*

He swallowed, hearing the desperation in her voice and fancied he could once again smell the acrid stench of pyre smoke. His breathing hitched in the back of his throat as unbidden, his eyes searched the dark for a friend he knew could not be there. The shadows blurred taking the shapes of toothy rocks against crashing, tumultuous waves.

An amorphous whimper escaped his lips, beneath the waves licking the bodies strung to their tips. Old blood and entrails leaked, turning the foam to foetid slurry.

*"Eremis,"* the voice called to him once again.

He shook his head and squeezed his eyes shut. "You are not real," he replied. His voice emanated from the very depths of his being. "You are a ghost, a haunting, a curse sent to condemn me."

*"A memory,"* the voice corrected. *"I am your friend."*

He opened his eyes in confusion. The voices had called and screamed inside his head but they had never replied. "To whom do I speak?" he asked tentatively.

*"I am Rosola, Watcher of the wild paths,"* the voice returned, like a melodious breeze through new grass.

Eremis swallowed again, wetting his cracked lips with the tip of his tongue. "That is not possible. Rosola is dead."

He could see her now. A spirit of slight limbs and smooth skin. Braids snaked down to her shoulders and writhed ceaselessly when she shook her head.

The stench of old blood and gore was overpowering and though he knew it could not be so, still he felt the cold flood water fill his boots, chilling him to the core. Looking around, Eremis saw that the surrounding shadows were full of eyes that burned with amber. He could make out their tortured bodies, curved like antlers.

"I am not the Eremis that you left behind," he muttered. "It is only his body that remains."

*"Great Warden,"* she said with urgency. *"That is a lie."*

"A bold claim," Eremis snorted, "from one who speaks to me from beyond the grave."

*"You are not the one who was left behind,"* the spirit chastised, her voice scratching like brittle twigs. *"Your actions bring death."*

His body shook at the insult and he turned away, trying to blot the sound of her voice from his mind.

*"Help us. Help them,"* she implored. *"I have never left your side. Do not abandon them as you once abandoned me."*

He crawled away from the shadows, the guilt gnawing at him as surely as his hunger. Part of him wanted to run from her but what remained of his sanity told him that there was no hole she would not find him, save one. He staggered to his feet. Bright painful bursts of light exploded behind his eyes. He moaned, a terrible soul-lost sound that echoed in a hundred different tones around him, each more painful than the last.

With one hand clutching the ragged cloak and the other feeling along the cave wall he walked towards the entrance.

"Eremis!" Rosola cried out as the clash of weapons and armour rose and fell close at hand. "Eroth's mercy! We are too late."

As the Watcher spoke, a man - a Drau, stumbled from the trees, an axe lodged in his shoulder. He fell face-first in to the foetid shallows of standing water. Beyond, screams and shouts echoed through the branches as the dispossessed scattered to the safety of the trees. Dark shapes followed in their wake, muscled and stocky.

The Dwentari roared like a beast as it broke upon them and pulled the blade of the axes from where it was embedded. Like a drunkard, it pushed away and trudged through the pool towards them, a dozen foreign curses upon his blackened lips. Others clambered in his wake, carrying the filth-smeared bodies of their spoils - some still struggling for life.

"Eroth's fangs!" Rosola called out, the snake-like braids of her hair squirming this way and that as she surveyed the closing forces arrayed against her. She reached for her bow as an arm pulled her back.

"You cannot take all of them," Eremis persuaded. He grabbed her into his arms, almost lifting her up in his haste to pull her away.

"They upset the balance," she retorted angrily, pulling herself free. "I will not stand to allow my kinsmen to be slaughtered like pigs."

He felt the fear and revulsion radiate from her like an aura as they retreated. She looked at him, the shock of the life taken before her was written in every crease of her face.

A call in an alien voice shattered the moment and Eremis dragged them both behind the dubious safety of a massive thornwood tree. They were the only force of note this far east. Watchers were nomadic and solitary for the most part. It had been necessity that had drawn them together.

Rosola was young and impetuous. She had been at the sacking of Esari and watched the Dwentari burn along the Mouth of Malinax like a plague locusts. Her ire was up and she desired nothing more than vengeance. It had almost cost her life. Eremis had found her half dead in the bowl of a tree, skewered with a trio of heavy iron crossbow bolts. By some miracle, none had burst her internal organs and she had returned to health with the speedy recovery of youth. Her brush with death had not lessened her ardour to deal it out.

The call came again, gruff yet strangely playful. He turned to her and placed a finger against his lips before inching his way to peer around the side of the tree. The lumpen shapes of the Dwentari were struggling towards them, their chitinous iron armour slowing them down. He pulled back.

"There are too many," he insisted with a whisper.

Rosola's face contorted into an angry snarl. "Those people will die if we do not provide them the opportunity of escape."

"They are already dead," Eremis replied, daring another look to check the enemies' progress. "It is four days to Fort Vheadari. They will not make it."

"They will not have the chance, if we do not help," she insisted, trying to push past. "I had no idea you were more fearful than they."

He arrested her, pushing her into the toughened bark of the tree. "I am not fearful. I am seasoned," he growled. "When I hunt I do not do so in the beast's own lair."

She scowled but stayed motionless. He eased his grip on her a fraction. Suddenly, her boot kicked out catching him in the knee. She tore herself away and darted out with banshee wail upon her lips. One, two, three arrows loosed one after the other.

Eremis cursed and willed himself to follow her, tearing free a silver hunter's blade from his waist. Roots tore and popped beneath his feet as he staggered and splashed in her wake.

The Dwentari yelled triumphantly at the sight of Rosola, heedless of it's own ally collapsing by its side, a tawny fletched arrow through its throat. It shouted to its other compatriots even as she descended upon it, wielding her bow like a mace. It ducked beneath the strike a moment before it might have been brained by the impact, and replied with one of its own. The gore-slicked axe whistling through the air in a decapitating strike. It stuck into the base of a petrified trunk, missing by a hair's breadth. The wood splintered and cracked as he tore it free with surprising force, hurtling it straight back for a second swing.

Rosola stumbled, surprised by the speed of it. Dancing out of the path of death, till with a snap, her foot caught between the latticed roots of a submerged sapling. The axe swung up again, angled for her skull. The roots would not release.

Eremis caught the impact against his blade with a scream of metal and shouldered the Dwentari off his feet and backwards into the water. It splashed and struggled to get back to its feet, shouting out to the others around it and waving a fat gauntleted hand in their direction. The other Dwentari charged, dropping their gains in favour of the greater challenge.

Rosola struggled to be free while Eremis fought for their lives. Drau were usually swift and agile, but the mud and stagnant water swamped his movements. The Dwentari trudged through the mire with indomitable certainty. Their blades cleaved through weeds and thorny bushes without being hindered. They set upon them like dogs, seemingly oblivious as other tantalizing targets fled into the forest, dragging their loved ones with them.

With a yell of victory, Rosola pulled herself free, using the spring of the sapling to leap up with a fluid grace. She ducked and weaved beneath the clumsy swings of Eremis's blade. Simply laying her hands upon the first Dwentari she could touch and snapping its neck with a deft twist.

Two of his grotesque companions waded towards them as she snatched up her bow floating in the water, and the pair pressed back to back. Rosola's eagle-eyed precision left a mire of sinking bodies to the left. While Eremis stretched out with his blade, moving with a dancers confidence. Stabbing, slashing, and shearing before sending their shattered remains out in one deadly sweep.

"We must retreat," Eremis insisted. "We cannot halt them any further," he continued, noticing more bulky shapes lumbering towards them.

"For Agrellon, for the Draurhegar!" Rosola shrieked at the top of her lungs, seemingly oblivious to the situation.

Drawn by the hope in her voice like moths to a flame, the Dwentari closed on them and began swinging their weapons, in a hurricane of blades and barbs.


Eremis shuffled, knees knocking, and hunched against the elements. His footprints left long drag marks against the sand and stone strewn runnel of the cliff-top path. A hundred feet below, the wreck of a Dwentari ship lay open to the elements, the waves licking and picking its exposed skeleton clean with each strike.

*"You are afraid."*

He twitched at the sound of the shade's voice, turning and seeing her familiar face in the sweep of the tall sea grass.

"I feel no fear," he shivered.

*"Yet you are hiding,"* she continued.

He turned quickly, his frail joints cracking at the sudden action. "Why do you haunt me spirit? What malign impulse insists you torture me this way?" His head turned this way and that, startled by the sound of his own voice.

A rumble of thunder replied to his yell, accompanied by the patter of heavy rain as the heavens opened above him. Then silence. He stumbled from the path breath issuing from between his cracked lips in small frigid puffs.

"Where are you?" he called, tearing away the tall lengths of grass as

if he could uncover her hiding spot. "Don't leave," he whimpered.
*"I never will."*
He cried out in terror as her voice seemed to whisper just behind his ear. Turning unsteadily, he tripped against a skull-sized stone and toppled, falling end over end down the gentle slope.

Eremis brought his free arm around in a whirling hay-maker, slamming it into the jaw of the nearest Dwentari irrespective of the snarling helm that covered it's face. A pair of muscle-slabbed shapes emerged to his right through a buzzing cloud of gnats and flies, their axes still dripping with blood from their recent butchery. As they waded towards him, he swung out, the blade cutting the air with a whisper. Corroded plate crumbled beneath the blow, toughened leather split, and blood welled from the wound. The Dwentari staggered back but did not fall, merely grunting a rebuke and smashing it's shoulder into Eremis's face.

He fell back, the scum from the water's surface coating his face with green algae. Like a rabid beast, the Dwentari leaped on him and his head once again submerged beneath the water, trapped beneath it's monstrous weight. The mud and pollutants stung his eyes. He thrashed madly, lungs aching for air. Blind and suffocating, he reached into the thick mud beneath him, fingers effortlessly churning through the rotting mulch till he found a stone and in one swinging motion, he smashed it against the head of his assailant.

The Dwentari stiffened and slumped to one side as Eremis burst up from the water, taking in great gasps of air. He had no time to catch his breath. The pool had become a charnel swamp of bodies and blood. Less than a foot away, Rosola still fought, standing over him like a mother bear protecting her cub. The irony was not lost on him. He heaved himself from the ground, loosely clutching his knife in one hand. Somewhere out beyond his sight, drums were beating. A base rhythm that grew forever louder. For a moment he was rooted to the spot - they could only do so much.

Suddenly, the undergrowth burst apart as a giant lizard tore through bark and branch as if it was nothing but paper. It hissed, serrated maw snapping at anything within reach. Eremis stumbled back in surprise. Two riders were mounted upon the creature's back, they struck and yanked at the iron links that bound the creature to their will. It thrashed its mighty limbs, splashing the filth and mud about it and with a bone-crushing swipe, Eremis was sent slamming into the nearest tree with the Dwentari warriors ready to chop him down.

"No!" Rosola yelled, dispatching the nearest one as effectively as possible and splashing through the shallows towards Eremis.

He coughed, feeling something pop in his chest by some miracle he was still holding his blade.

She placed a hand on his shoulder, her face coated in blood not her own. He reached out and shoved her aside. A torn-faced warrior stomped through the swamp towards them, it's face a mess of ritual scarification, but Rosola seized his blade from his fingertips and took out its legs with a spinning swipe. As it splashed back into the water, she leaped atop of him stabbing down again and again with a series of vicious strikes.

Eremis mustered what strength had not been knocked out of him and stood, his vision blurred and the pain in his chest felt as if his lungs were on fire. Seizing his blade back from Rosola's outstretched hand he pulled her back before the monster's wrath.

"Get down," he gasped.

For once, Rosola did as commanded, the seriousness of his tone forcing even her bright spirit to compliance. She dropped, kneeling in the disgusting waters.

Eremis whispered to the blade and swung outwards, clutching Rosola to him. The blade hissed across the air trailing a silver haze, it passed over the bodies of the still-standing Dwentari, their heavy armour offering no protection. Soon, the trees rang with fresh screams both monster and humanoid alike. Flesh parted. Some warriors were shared in half by the passage of glittering light as bright as a full moon, their rank innards displayed for all to see. Those too close simply came apart in a rain of gore.

Eremis did not wait to behold the devastation. He reached out for Rosola and dragged her to her feet, shoving her ahead of him as he turned and fled.

"Run!" he urged, stumbling as best he could against the pain. "For the love of Eroth, run!"

"But the people," Rosola gasped, wading as fast as she could between the gnarled roots of the trees.

"No time," he pressed. "Their lives are in their own hands as are ours at this moment. We must make for higher ground and hope that they do not follow."

*"Get up Eremis."*

The sky was dotted with starlight. He didn't know for how long he had been staring up at them. Hours seemed meaningless.

*"Get up."* The voice was urgent, almost angry. *"We must make for higher ground."*

He shook his head. "That was another time."

Broken fingernails clawed at the grass as he tried to sit up, but the throbbing pain of his skull would not allow it. He reached up and gingerly touched his head. His fingers came away sticky with slowly coagulating blood.

*"You are not dead yet. It is not your blood that salts the earth."*

Slowly, Eremis turned on his side and curled into a foetal shape. "It was not my fault. I meant no harm."

*"Few do,"* the spirit soothed. *"Yet here we are."*

"Please," he begged, fingers wrapped into the grass like a security blanket. "Stop."

*"Get up. We are not done."*

As if compelled by some higher purpose and clenching his jaw against the pain, Eremis dragged himself to his feet and staggered like a wooden puppet into the night.

The closer then crept to the town of Esari, the more torched and mutilated the forest became. Trees were bare, blackened and abloom with fungi. Through the leafless canopy and shorn branches, Eremis saw the ground begin to rise towards a rocky mound, the first dry ground they'd seen since descending to the forest floor. The mighty tree that had once crowned it's top was now nothing more than a stump. It's wood carted away for fuel or perhaps repairs for the Dwentar army. Beaten and sore, they crested the hillock and looked down into the valley that lead to the coast. There in the intervening gap, the red glare of fires flickered against the darkness. The Dwentari had made their camp within the ruins of Esari, engaged in whatever dread ceremonies their superiors saw fit to celebrate with.

Unable to move further, Eremis slumped to the ground. There was no way ahead. With the raiding party behind them and the bulk of the Dwentari force ahead, they were caught like rabbits in a snare.

Rosola slithered on her stomach to the top of the crest, keeping her head low. "They have more prisoners," she murmured and looked back at him expectantly.

He sighed and pulled himself back to his feet.

"You're going to fight them?" she said, her voice alight with hope.

He gave her a look and began to shuffle wearily back down the mound.

"They must be purged," she insisted.

"We cannot save them," he replied.

"We saved the ones in the forest," she countered. "Some of them at least must have got away."

He nodded. "And now we are caught between two blades." He pointed to a small copse of trees still standing in the valley below. "Perhaps, if we can make it to those, we might escape with our own skin."

"I swore to defend this land," Rosola hissed angrily. "I was there when they..."

"We swore to slay the monsters," Eremis interjected. "But, this is no mere monster. It is a hydra. For every head that you take, two more will grow and you have neither the means nor the arms to defeat it alone."

"Then stand with me," she pleaded, darting past to stand in his way. "I will not dishonour my name by allowing the land I swore to keep, fall to the beasts."

"Then you will die or be captured and the time I took to bring you from the brink of death will have been for nothing." He shook his head in disagreement but the desperation in her eyes cut him as sure as any blade. His face softened to a sad smile. "I commend your courage. I cannot fault you for wanting to honour the oaths you spoke to the council at Agrellon. But this?" He gestured outwards. "This is suicide."

He reached out for her but she shrank away from his touch.

"You are old," she spat angrily. "You have lost your taste for the hunt."

Now it was Eremis's turn to feel anger. It burned like a freshly lit torch. "I have lived this long by wit and wisdom alone," he snarled, "and I will not have you jeopardise my life with your need for glory. You would do well to remember that."

Rosola started away from him, shocked by his sudden outburst. Regaining her composure, she folded her arms. "Very well. I will court your shadow Old Man, till we reach the fort. Perhaps the local lord will have more stomach for blood than you."

Eremis sighed but did not rise to the bait.

They slunk down the hillside, the ground once again growing steadily more boggy the lower they went, stalking the shadows like a pair of phantoms. It was no small task. The fires of the encampment lengthened and shorted the patches of darkness at irregular intervals, missteps were inevitable and they could only hope that if anyone was watching, they happened to look the other way.

Like a terrifying entity of the hells, the firelight suddenly raged brightly, sending them skittering backwards from its light. Fire's stoked across the camp and voices rang out amid the crackle of the flames. Strange tongues drifted on the wind, a language that neither Eremis nor Rosola could understand, though the intent was clear. These were celebrations. A feast over a victory assured.

Rosola swore under her breath.

"Ignore them," Eremis warned. "Let them dance the night away if they wish. By morning we will be well on our way and they will not be our concern." He slithered on his stomach, arm over arm, ignoring the searing pain of what he was sure now, must be a broken rib. Grinding his teeth against the pain he inched closer towards the thicket.

She followed him, her sinewy form making light work of it.

Gurgling laughter echoed from the camp's interior followed by a high pitched scream and a call for mercy. Rosola froze, her head snapping towards the sound. Squinting against the light, she could make out shapes. The scruffy silhouettes surrounding a leaner, lither form that they tossed and jostled like a toy. The Dwentari seemed to find a madness and hilarity in another's suffering. While their victim tried desperately to escape their bully circle, they belly-laughed and roared above the pleas for help.

She turned and looked at Eremis. The older watcher was shaking his head. "There is nothing you can do," he mouthed at her.

Heart thundering inside her chest, she tried to turn away. But, the pitiful cries seemed to hold her in place.

Eremis caught the contest of wills in her eyes. He shook his head again and gestured impatiently to the rising copse of trees. *Don't do it,* he thought. *Leave them to their fate.*

Another scream was cut brutally short by the sound of a fist and Rosola shut her eyes but she could not leave. Sliding her bow from her back she turned and ran towards the camp.

By the time that the Dwentari realised that the Watcher was upon them, it was too late. Rosola had her short bow in hand and had loosed half-a-dozen arrows into their midst. Like a terrifying spirit of the forest, she shot arrow after arrow into the group with such force that they were flung back skewered and squealing, leaving those that remained to scatter into the camp.

The Drau woman was already dead. He face was crumpled in no one side. What exactly had her, remained a mystery, for there was little of her left-hand skull save bone shards and brain matter. Across the camp, it was slowly dawning on the Dwentari that they were under attack. Some had been sleeping in a drunken stupor, while others had removed their weapons and plate the better to enjoy the spoils of war. Rosola made them bleed for their lack of discipline. Their suffering was swift, as she sent one after another into sweet oblivion, tearing out and reusing her arrows as she went. Somewhere in the dark beyond the fires, she could still hear Eremis yelling her name.

Warriors that had moments before been engaged in raucous, brotherly celebration, scrabbled for weapons. Their leader shook himself awake and managed to grasp his weapon only to take an arrow to the throat before his lips could issue a single order. As she worked around the fire, more Dwentari warriors charged at her, taking a ground shaking charge. She laughed and brained the first that reached her with the spiked butt of her bow, tripping the second with an outstretched leg and sending them diving into the flames of their own camp fire. Limbs flailed and the smell of cooked meat filled the air as the warrior was consumed by the inferno. It was almost too easy.

Too caught up in the rapture of her well earned justice, she did not see the blade come down behind her.

"Rosola!"

She turned towards the fire, surprised to hear Eremis's voice so close, the braids of her hair whipping the side of her face. Her eyes went wide to see him leap through the embers of the flames as if birthed like a phoenix, blade outstretched.

The barbed sword hammered down against her, tearing away her leather armour and chewing into her skin as if it was nothing. She tumbled to her knees, heat blossoming across her back and neck, blinking and stunned. For a moment her vision swam in and out of darkness, fleeting shadows as the blade rose up once more for a second strike. She watched it fall.

The ring of metal on metal sang loud and clear as Eremis twisted the attack out of its decapitating strike. The teeth of the blade caught against the silvered edge of his own, screaming a handful of sparks as both edges fought for superiority.

Eremis yelled in pain as an iron capped boot sent him sprawling backwards. He rolled to miss the roaring flames of the fire. Breath catching in his throat from the smoke, he glanced around looked for Rosola. He spied her, doggedly staggering towards the wicker cage that held the prisoners. *Eroth's teeth, if her stubborn determination wouldn't be the end of them both!*

The boot slammed onto his chest, knocking the air out of him with a scream of pain. He looked up into the face of his attacker. The Dwentari, seemed impossibly big as he leered over Eremis's prone form. Bright eyes glittered behind a torrent of matted course hair woven with metal rings and bone fetishes. It snarled something down to him, foul spittle spraying from between its bulbous lips. For a second, the Dwentari's attention was accosted by the sound of many running feet. Seizing his opportunity, Eremis reached for his blade. A second foot came down on the flat of it. The silvered steel bent, moaned and shattered, the snapped hilt releasing into his grasp. Above him, the warrior burbled with laughter and waggled a fat finger down at him.

Eremis stared for what seemed like eternity and the splintered hilt of his most beloved possession. A Watcher's weapon was almost a holy relic. Each was individual, paired only to it's wielder. Singular. To see it destroyed before his eyes was akin to having his heart pulled out through his chest. In fact, such a torture would have been preferable. As his senses came rushing back, instinct took over. Terror. A fear of death and without hesitation, he sank what little remained for the blade right down to the hilt, through the ankle of his attacker.

The Dwentari recoiled, bawling in pain as he withdrew the blade. He rolled coughing and panting, struggling on to his feet. Dozens of ragged Drau, young and old, were fleeing the camp. Haphazardly he searched for Rosola for a few precious seconds, before his attacker roared its challenge, defiantly hobbling towards him. He turned and fled, hoping that Rosola was long gone with the other escapees.

"The trees! Head for the trees!" voices shouted at random. "Flee! Run for your lives!"

Eremis was buffeted by the stampede like a leaf tossed in a gale. Arms reached out, pulling him back in their haste to forge ahead. He watched horrified as an elder backhanded a female to the floor while she clasped her wailing babe to her chest. A child toppled over the lumpen turf and yelled in pain as she was trampled into the mud. He pushed against the crowd, scooping up the struggling child before herd instinct could see the end of her. She screamed and clawed at his face, no longer able to tell friend from foe. He dropped her and she ran into the throng.

A hand touched his shoulder. He spun, ready to take on anyone who would do him harm with tooth and nail if necessary. Only by the will of Eroth herself did he manage to prevent himself from slicing through the throat of Rosola behind him. She stumbled back from the blow, catching herself before she could fall. Blood leaked from the corner of her mouth and from a split lip, coating her teeth and gums as she tried to smile. She was pale as the winter's sun and shuffled with a pronounced limp. He caught her as she pressed towards him, using her bow as a walking stick.

"What have you done?" he asked, shaking her roughly. "Look what has come down upon us." He turned her roughly to point at the swiftly mustering Dwentari forces. "They will run us down like animals." He did not wait for her response, turning and forging ahead in the direction of the trees.

The wind whipped and whined as Eremis dragged his aching body to the top of the next valley. The land stretched out before him like an endless churning sea of slopes and ridges. Small groves of thornwood trees clustered like freckles upon it, their thick branches be-speckled with leaves. He sunk to his knees on the soft grass, so tired he could barely keep his eyes open.

She was always with him now. Her incessant nattering persistent and enduring. If he squinted he could see her no matter the light. Her face was carved into the patterned bark of the trees, the trapped light between leaves, and the skipping stones of bubbling brooks. She was as much a part of the land as of his own fantasies.

*"Behold the endless nothing that awaits you."*

Once again her voice slipped into condescending tones laced with a malice that chilled his heart. Yet, he shook his head. "You are wrong spirit. I know what lies beyond these hills. The Draurhegar have not yet been defeated. I know it."

*"Yes, great guardian. You know much of defeat."*

His breath rattled in his chest as he closed his eyes. "There was no choice," he moaned.

*"Life is always a choice."*

He could feel her on the back of his neck, soft like morning mist. He turned, half expecting to see her there. "Why are you doing this to me? Can't you see the daily torture I endure? I saved your life. Have you no words of comfort to salve this madness?"

*"You weaned me as a farmer does a new-born calf and I grew fat off your honeyed words."*

He leaned against the nearest tree, shaking. "No," he cried.

*"And when the time came..."*

His fingernails pushed into the bark, tearing across it's surface. "No," he repeated, banging his head in bid to banish her.

*"You sold us to slaughter."*

The nails tore and bled.

*"Fear not my noble Watcher. For I will not abandon you as you did them. I will be forever at your side. You will not face the slow years alone."*


Under the cover of bare and twisted branches, the group took refuge but they could not do so for long. What little light the moon had shone was gone, mother night had suffocated it behind a blanket of stormy clouds. The darkness would hinder the Dwentari in their pursuit but it would not stop them. Their blood was up and they would seek recompense for the butchery of their comrades. The people about Eremis were packed tight, huddled together in their joint suffering. Voices rose and fell, back and forth, as they sought solace in knowing that they were not alone, or at the very least, that there were plenty of bodies to offer up in the event of their discovery.

Eremis stumbled from trunk to trunk as he made his way through the sea of warm figures, till he came upon Rosola. She looked up at him as he approached with caution. Dirty, white wrappings were wound around her torso and she was easing what was left of her armour over the top, wincing with every flex of her shoulders.

"What more can you possibly have to say to me?" she hissed through the pain.

"It was a foolish decision," he nodded. "You must be aware that we cannot escort all of them to the fort and remain undetected."

"Then we must take them as far as we can," she growled and stood wobbling against the stick of her bow. "It is our duty to give them a fighting chance."

Eremis shook his head. "It is not our duty but you have made it so." He held up a hand, seeing her eyes flash with sudden anger. "I have not come to argue."

"Then why are you pestering me?" She brushed past him, knitting her way through the worn and weary.

"Because I would not see you destroy yourself," he replied, following in her wake.

Rosola stopped and turned, leaning in towards him. "Less than an hour ago, you had already decided that these people were not worth saving. Less than an hour ago you challenged my right to defend the wards to which I had been assigned," she murmured, her voice little more than a dangerous whisper.

"You were reckless. You saw glory and honour in the flames and you went for them," he argued.

She looked at him with murderous wrath. "Every life is worth saving," she replied, drawing herself up to her full height despite the obvious pain it must have cost her. "Even yours, or I would not have protected you in the pool."

Eremis looked away, a twinge of shame lodging itself uncomfortably in his brain. "There is a bridge across the cove," he began changing the topic of conversation. "It could shorten our journey by days."

"Why did you not speak of it before?" Rosola asked.

"Because it will lead us across open ground where we are easy prey," he sighed, "and because I thought I could make you see reason."

She looked at him scornfully. "We will make for this bridge you speak of. We have out run them so far. We will continue to do so."

Eremis looked around at the sorrowful and exhausted faces around him in doubt. They were tired, hungry, and scared. They did not bear the countenance of the guerilla fighters she spoke of. Many looked like they would not survive the elements, let alone a night's march across field and fen.

A female elder reached out and touched his leg, her smile was contorted by an ugly black and purple bruise. "We are stronger than we look," she croaked. "Wherever you lead, Watcher, we will follow."

The sky opened. The column stretched out for fifty feet in a long if somewhat lumpen serpent but it was growing longer by the hour. Rosola cut an impressive pace despite her limp, striding across the fenland, seemingly oblivious to the wretched moans and suffering of her fellow travellers. They would reach The Mouth before dawn, she told them. Only then, when the sea parted them from their pursuers would she slow the pace. Till then they simply must keep going.

As the patches of woodland thinned to patchy mounds of rock and grass, there seemed to be no part of the land he had once known that had not been tainted by the mark of the Dwentari. The willowy trees had been shattered to their stumps and where once seas of tall grasses had once spread, now only a muddy mire expanded. Once, this plain had supported migrating herds of wild creatures. The air had sung with the murmur of insects. The wild grandeur of it was gone, rotted away beneath the footsteps of the enemy that stalked them. Now, the land darkened, shivered, and quaked like a fever afflicted body.

By the time they reached the standing stones that rose like broken teeth at the first reaches of The Mouth, they were soaked and coated head to toe in mud. They resembled a marching army of golems and they were slow. Time and again Rosola walked back along the line, urging them to pick up the pace, promising them that the end of this trial was just beyond the next rise. Yet, despite the steady crawl of time, the Dwentari were not seen behind them.

"Stop," Eremis instructed, placing a hand out against her chest. "Look."

Ahead, barely visible against the night, a pack of wolves darted across the plane. Faint howls echoing into the dark.

"What of it?" she asked, calling a halt to the march in the windswept curve of a tall rise. "We are too large a prey for them. They will not bother us. Even with my wounds, I am more than a match for any wolf."

He shook his head, eyes darting for the slightest bit of movement. "I don't like it. What are they hunting? There is nothing here for them."

Rosola shrugged. "The natural balance has been disturbed, perhaps they are simply trying to survive as much as us." She pointed across to the far side of the vale. "The Mouth," she said simply but there was a note of relief in her voice. "We have nearly reached your bridge."

He held her firm as she tried to walk past. "Listen," he hissed. "Can't you hear that?"

She stopped and held her breath for a few moments before shaking her head. "You are dreaming. I hear nothing."

"Something is not right. Even the wolves have stopped." He looked at her. "We should turned back, head inland."

"The bridge is right there!" Rosola exasperated, her voice rising.

Murmurs began to vibrated along the column. Eremis looked back at them and place a finger to his lips. "Hush. You will make them panic." He forced a smile to his lips, giving the nearest a nod and dragging her a few feet out of ear shot.

"I have not lived this long by accident. My instincts are screaming at me to be gone from this place," he insisted.

"Then let us be gone," she replied. "It is you that is delaying." She turned back and raised her voice. "There is bridge on the far side," she announced to a reception of mutters and questions. "Once we are over it, we can all rest." Sighs of relief punctuated the low hum of chatter. She turned, giving Eremis a stern look and the column moved on with renewed vigour.

As they hugged the rise of the hill, Eremis found that this gully hung over the fen like a petrified wave. The gulley it formed, offered a natural protection against the worst of the elements. There were signs that they had not been the first. A dispossessed shoe here, a torn cloth there. Something small and white floated in a puddle ahead. He scooped down and picked it up. It was a small toy, a cat perhaps, carved from whale bone and no bigger than the palm of his hand. His instincts rattled as he clutched the small figurine, like chalk on tile. His hand drifted by habit to the hilt of his shattered blade, a mote of courage spreading through him from the feel of the cold metal at his finger tips. He took another step, his boots squelching in the soft mud. Something cracked beneath his weight.

At first he thought it just a twig or rotten brunch that had sunk beneath the earth. Water belched and burped as he dislodged it before just as suddenly hurling back into the night, his entire body shaking in shock. It was a femur. A scream suddenly erupted from further back in the column and a female picked herself up from the ground, her fingers locked in the eye sockets of a broken skull. Soon she was joined by others as slowly, other items were discovered. A rib, a clavicle, the vertebrae links of a spine. Fear spread lightening quick through the column, like poison though a man's veins. People began to pull away from each other.

An undulating call, shattered the heavy air. Nothing natural that Eremis had heard of, had ever made a sound like that.

"What in the hells was that?" Rosola, limped to his side. Her movement was so restricted now that Eremis feared her wound had become infected in their travels.

The people were scattering, their resolve broken, the last shards of their courage atomised. She turned, yelling at them to stay together, but survival instinct had taken hold. Another call sent them into panic, followed by another and another, till the air vibrated with the strange, sorrowful sound.

"Eroth have mercy!" Eremis whispered, catching the flicker of torch light across the ridge, spreading across its length like wildfire. Without another word he turned and ran.

The sky flickered with the crackle of lightening, briefly illuminating the war-torn battle field. Lurching poles that had previously appeared to be malformed saplings now stood to be bent and broken spears. In that flash of brightness the glamour that had held them was cast aside to reveal the true horror they had unwittingly stumbled in to.

High on the ridge the fanged maws of the Dwentari cavalry drooled and hissed, snapping at each other with barely held restraint and with one final wailing call, the horde descended upon them, clawing their way down the vertical divide as if it were little more than open ground. Each beast towered five feet from nose to ground and at least twice that in length. Before long, they had reached cleft of the base, tooth and claw smashing a path through bone and blood in abandon. Guided by the sounds of screams the second riders slid from the backs of their mounts, picking their way through the corpses and sweeping upon their half-dead foes.

"Stay together," Rosola insisted, screaming at the top of her lungs. "Don't let them pick you off one by one." But, the field was a charnel house and none were listening.

Eremis dodged and darted between monsters and men. The lizard-beasts bludgeoned and swiped gasping victims to the ground, smashing them into the blood-soaked mud. He ducked as an axe whirred above his head and cleaved into the skull of some poor elder and the old Drau did his best to flee. He fell and his body was snatched by a passing lizard, brittle bones meaning little in creatures immense jaws.

The Dwentari fought with indomitable fervour, rank after rank of warriors and beasts gladly walking up to their ankles in bloody-slick body parts and pulverised bone. Eremis tried to block out their sickening cheers, concentrating on living.

"Stay close," Rosola called to the half dozen individuals whose mind had not yet been consumed by terror. They wielded rocks and broken spears looted from the battlefield. "We make for the bridge," she added, cracking the skull of the nearest Dwentari that got close. They were swamped by bodies. Horned-frilled beasts were loosed from their chains, loping across the battlefield, attempting to smash to pulp anything that got in their way. Rosola struck out again, smashing her bow like a club into on of its elephantine limbs, even as its claws clipped the head from the shoulders of the Drau next to her.

Rosola charged at the monster, almost tripping over her own feet as she slammed her body into its own. It's Cyclopean eye rolled in its socket, stunned by the ferocity of the attack. She stabbed down at the thing with the spiked end of her bow, ripping furiously into its swollen belly, tearing the rancid guts out of the creature.

The monster raged like a demon. It would not be stopped.Grabbing her with unnatural strength, the beat tossed her back into her would-be allies, knocking them back like a set of garden skittles.

She yelled in pain, feeling a muscle tear and her shoulder pop under the impact. Desperately, she struggled to remove herself from the tangle of flailing limbs. She pulled herself free, rolling back in mire and spitting mud from her mouth.

"Eremis?" she called, seizing the first fleeing captive she could lay hands upon. "Where is Eremis?"

The terrified male shoved her away with a curse.

Suddenly, something gave. The sky to the lit up with light. The hordes of the Dwentari had descended upon them, but in truth their attack was as blind as they were. Now, however, bright balls of flame were hurled high into the air from some infernal source still bound to the ridge. Upon the ridge itself, mouldering barrels of black pitch and oil were smashed open, their contents sent to flood down into the trap below. As the hurling balls of flame found their mark, the tar rivers burst into life destroying anything caught within a few feet of them and rendering all to ash and bone.

Now in this new light, struggling back from the force of the blast, Eremis could see that this was not the only reinforcement. Walking mountains of corpulent serpents were making their way toward them. A jubilant cry arose from the Dwentari and he withdrew, crawling backwards against the sludge as one such beast turned, fixating its baleful glare upon him.

It took a moment for Eremis to realise that the scream was his own. He flopped onto his front, flapping and wallowing through the mud like a landed fish. "Eroth, save me!" he whispered over and over again as a mantra till he was breathless with exertion. He spat and swallowed the congealed mud and matter as it slopped across his face, blocking his nose and blinding his eyes. He tried to struggle to his feet, his boots feeling like they had been filled with lead weights. They slipped and skidded beneath him. The cacophony of the massacre was deafening. He could barely think and as the ragged lower half of some poor soul, hammered into the ground in front of him, he was thankful for that.

"The bridge!"

Eremis looked up at the sound of the shout, seeing a dozen or so individuals pushing and falling over each other in their haste to reach the scruff of bushes and wiry rope bridge on the far side. He glanced around, noticing that he was not the only one to have heard the call. Suddenly his legs seemed sure. Hope, salvation, the chance to live, flooded through his muscles granting them new strength.

The bridge was in poor shape, little more than hope and dreams held its rotten planks and frayed cord together. He thundered onto it, barely contemplating the hundreds of feet that stretched between him the knife-edge rocks that speared from the water below. It stretched from one side of the cove to the other and was swinging wildly. Each pendulum swell causing it to creak and crack.

Eremis hammered across the first few feet, till with a snap, the plank beneath his foot disintegrated. He toppled, grasping for the at what ever he could get his hands on before he was thrown over the edge. His hands caught on to a leg and he yelled out as the boot attached kicked into his face.

"Get off me!" the stricken Drau cried, desperate to release his foot and remain balanced.

The bridge swung as others tried to push past. Desperate to escape the boot kicked again and something crunched painfully inside.

"Let go! You will kill as both," he continued.

Eremis let go as the third kick collided with his temple. The Drau gave a scream, surprised by the sudden release and lost his balance, toppling head of heel from the bridge till his wail was consumed by the sea below. Shouts of alarm followed him into the dark.

"Stop!" Rosola's voice cut through the pain of his injuries like a surgeons blade. "Desist, or I will kill you all myself," she panted breathlessly and pointed the end of her bow at the nearest to her. "Let the Watcher cross. There will be one of us at each end. The bridge will not withstand all of us at once. If you try, the bridge will collapse and you will doom us all." A glutinous, almost avian screech tore her attention away as a massive sack of flesh, struck the ground some way behind her. He caught her look as she glanced back at him. "Go," it read. "Run."

Eremis heaved himself unsteadily onto the planks, stretching his arms out like a tight-rope walker. Spots of darkness clustered at the corner of his vision, threatening to devour him. Behind he could still catch snatches of the combat that had taken hold.

"I will smash your foul form to splinters beast," Rosola shrieked madly, hefting the haft of her bow once again. The pain across her back blinding her to any fear this creature might have held over her. "I will send your foul presence to the abyss."

Its talon snatched out to catch her but she leaped from it's path and slammed the soul-wood of her bow against its gnarled flesh. The creature's booming call rolled across the battlefield. Such an attack might have given a casual beast of the forest pause, but the war-monsters of the Dwentari were bred with unnatural resilience and they feared their masters more than a terrified cluster of sinewy Drau. It coiled in on itself, like a viper preparing to strike.

Eremis reached the other side of the cove, tumbling into the soft unspoiled grass with a gasp. His heart was hammering so hard he thought it might burst from his chest and his face was already swelling with bruising. The bliss of escape was short lived. A series of yells and screams were deafened by cackle of the creature that leaped on the survivors the other side. Pulling himself to his feet, he watched it pounce on them, shaking them to bloody chunks like feral cat.

Others were now attempting the bridge, carefully making their way towards him but his eyes were fixated on the vulture-like creature that towered across the other side.

"Go," Rosola commanded, ushering the survivors one at a time, narrowly missing being torn to pieces herself. "Steady now, no pushing."

The creature thrashed, angered to see its playthings attempting to leave. It looked up and fixated its gaze upon the escape of its prey.

Eremis stared at the monster, suddenly aware of his presence - or so he thought. Behind those eyes stoked the fires of a monstrous intelligence that should never have been found in such a beast. Even here he felt he could sense the ground rattle beneath its weight and smell the rank stench of decomposing meat upon its breath. It had lost its interest in the small thing that danced around in front of it, its malevolence focused on another prize.

The whimper caught in his throat as Eremis stumbled back a step caught by the creatures gaze. The intensity of it shook him to the core. It reached out, a single talon crashing against the far side of the bridge, sending a shock wave along its surface. Someone fell.

"Eroth," he whispered, barely able to muster the word as his hand fell shaking to his hilt and tore what was left of his blade from the scabbard, wielding it before him with shaking hands. The light from the fires across the bridge, shimmered and danced across its still razor sharp edge. Without even thinking about what he was doing, Eremis launched at the stake that pinned the bridge to the other side and began hacking at the rope.

"Eremis," Rosola shouted as the bridge suddenly sagged. Realizing the sudden peril of his actions. "Eremis, what are you doing?!"

He could not hear her. He could only hear the scream of every nerve and synapse telling him to do whatever it took to stop that thing from coming near. *Live*, it told him and he obeyed. He hacked again and again at the toughened cords, the silvered edge of the shattered blade scoring through dozens of fibres at a time.

"Please, stop!" The shouts only made him word faster until with a whine and a snap the cord sheared, tearing the stake out of the ground and whipping his torso with its sudden release.

The tension of the bridge went slack. Rosola looked in shock as it and all of its occupants dropped like iron bricks into the dark.

"What have you done!" She mouthed, looking up in time to see Eremis flee into the dark. She turned and stared up into the embrace of death and the scream of her demise echoed long into the night.

Crows cawed from tops of moss covered rocks. The stone tower was shattered, its body scattered across the valley in chunks as if smote by Eroth herself. The Dwentari had already been here, he knew they would have. The fort was nothing now but a mortuary for the unburied dead.

He had hoped that there might have been some respite here, that her spirit might be inclined to leave him and seek out her own kind. It was wishful thinking. She remained at his side, always whispering, always a reminder, splintering his memory with every painful detail. He could not even focus on the words now.

The wooden branch of the gnarled tree creaked, the split leather of his belt snapped under tension, and something cracked. Then the world was plunged into darkness.

*Beneath the Skin*

"There is something at work in my soul, which I do not understand."
　　　　　　　　　　　　-Mary Shelley, Frankenstein

Urden drew his coat around him as he stepped from the shadows of the alley, his boots splashing through mud and night-soil. Iron grey skies threatened more rain before day's end. The garment was already soaked and the thick wool was a corpse weight on his shoulders. It had once been finely made. Accents of it's faded grandeur still clung to it: a silver button here, a frayed brocade there, but it was now stitched with more patches than the original fabric.

A shaft of waning sunlight pierced from between the clouds, turning puddles blood red. The village was already a hell scape. Dwentari soldiers had rampaged through here not a month past, but Skelda had not recovered and likely never would. The skeletal frames of houses still smelled of smoke, their shattered frames reaching for the sky like tortured finger bones. Even though most of the raiding party had moved on, Urden was nervous to be out in the streets alone. Thieves and cut-throats had claimed the village, steadily picking them clean like vultures at a carcass.

Nervously, he clutched the small knife in his pocket and darted to the shelter of the lengthening shadows. There had been four of them. Soren had been taken with a bolt to the back. Gerette had withered away before their eyes with shivering sickness. Then there had just been Urden and Isola. For a week, the pair of them hadn't dared to creep outside the house but the supplies had run down and after many tears, Isola had put on her scarf and raced out the door.

Urden missed his sister. She could take care of herself of that he was certain, but these were dangerous times and he wasn't sure his mind would bare to lose another so close to him. *I promise I'll come back.* He could still hear her say. *There is water in the tun and bread on the shelf. I won't go too far. Just to the farm and back.* She'd made it sound easy. As if it could be like that, as if it could be so ordinary. Perhaps it was simply that night had crept up on her and she had decided to take refuge rather than dare to be caught after dark.

Maybe the rain had caused the small river to flood and she had needed to find another way back. She should be back right now and wondering why he had left. So many possibilities and yet Urden could not shake the feeling that something else had happened, that there was a reason she had not returned.

He was not entirely alone. The village still lived - just. A few humans and children scurried to finish their business before darkness came. Each were thin and gangly. The Dwentari had seized most of the food. What little they had missed was hard to come by and those desperate enough had no qualms about murdering each other for a rind of cheese. If anyone had too much, they were likely to be killed by their own starving relatives. There was a rumour that some had taken to eating each other but Urden was sure that couldn't be true - could it?

A perpetual haze of old smoke hugged Skelda's streets. It was as if the village had died but it's tortured spirit refused to leave. The road opened out into the market square. Torn fabric awnings fluttered from broken stalls. No hawkers called out their wares, only the subdued murmur of frightened conversation cut shot at his approach. It was not wise to draw attention to oneself. Though he was confident that none here considered him any great threat, there were others who stalked the ruins hungrier then himself and more deadly. To linger was to find an early grave.

Now that Urden had reached the square, he relaxed a little. He could count maybe five or six other survivors and there was safety in numbers. Though local thugs had carved bits of the village and it's surroundings up for themselves, the square was considered neutral territory. Perhaps that was because they respected the small shrine of Eroth at it's centre, more likely it was simply that there was nothing left of worth. There was still a market here in a way. Citizens who had something of worth tried to sell them for old coins long since bereft of value - or services. Of the two, barter was preferred. Soft skin and living flesh had a tangible value that cold metal worn by touch did not. Though the number of these 'merchants' varied, there was always one that Urden could rely on being there.

Xenath Rosseren claimed that there was nothing he could not get. He had taken up residence in the largest, still standing structure, advertising himself as an impartial middle man and he did not take 'no' for an answer. Isola had sold their mother's pearls to him for a few days of food and night of fuel for the fire. He was an aggressive merchant, a Drau many years older than her. When she had returned, her face had been ash white and she'd vowed never to go near him again.

Urdan had been accosted by Xenath several times and detested him, but the drau had an uncanny ability to know things others did not, and if there was anyone who might be able to tell him something about Isola's whereabouts it would be him.

The merchant was haggling with an elderly woman over a basket. "What do mean rags? I walked for half a day to get them. They were pulled straight from the manor. See how soft the velvet is? Surely it must stretch to more than a few pieces of bread and a cut of pork!" the woman grumbled, holding up the arm of a dress for inspection. Her face was masked with desperation.

Xenath gave the stitching a pull followed by a well rehursed sigh. Urdan looked away and waited for their business to finish. He had seen this performance replayed a dozen times. When the woman left, clutching four small loaves to her chest and spitting curses, he approached Xenath's stall.

It was little more than a grave-robbers hoard. The Drau's face twisted into a wide smile as Urdan stepped up to the bench. Taller than him by at least a head, his elongated ears peaked out from oily black hair. Like most of his kind, his looks were strikingly sharp, in a better light, some might have called him handsome.

"Urdan! Come! Please, step-forward, don't be shy!" he called so loudly it made Urdan wince. "What brings you to my stall? You looked soaked through. Perhaps I can interest you in some new clothes." Xenath held out a familiar looking basket. "These just came in. Fit for a noble I'd wager."

Urdan waved the basket away. "Have you seen Isola?" he asked, getting straight to the point. "Did she pass through here?"

Xenath folded his arms, the steel blue of his eyes twinkling. "I usually see her a fair bit. Scampering off some place, keeping her head down. Why? Hasn't she come home?"

He didn't want to tell the drau the truth but he sorely needed something to go on. "She was on her way to the farm. I haven't seen her since yesterday." He muttered. Xenath's face filled with mocking concern. "Do you think something might have happened to her? I mean a mongrel like Isola might be seen as easy pickings if she was seen there."

Urdan bristled at the insult. Half-born, mongrel, bastard - whatever the drau wanted to call them, he would have to swallow it. "Do you know anything?" he pleaded quietly.

Xenath leaned against the bench. "I can't say that I have. I was here from dawn till dusk yesterday and I didn't even see her pass through."

Urdan felt his stomach lurch, painfully empty. If anyone had seen her, surely Xenath's eyes would have been all over her. The idea that Isola could have been snatched before she had reached the square suddenly seemed very likely.

"I could make some enquiries." Xenath added, leaning in. His breath stank of old wine. "What will you give me if I can find her?"

And there it was. Urden had anticipated that the sly drau would want something. Slowly he pulled the knife from his pocket. It was well made, silver edged, and engraved with coiled serpents fighting over the tiny piece of jasper affixed to the hilt.

Xenath appraised it for a few moments and then pushed it back. "Let's say by chance I can get Isola back for you. That'll cost more than your shiny toy. She's a pretty girl for her kind, perhaps we can come to an arrangement that would be more worthy of my time."

Urdan recoiled, unable to keep his anger in check. "I'd rather murder her myself than sell her out to you!" the drau shrugged, un-fazed. "As you see fit. Life is too short, especially if you are a young girl lost and alone." He smiled. "If you change your mind, you know where to find me."

Urden looked at him furiously, wanting so badly to punch that smug look off of his face. Drau were light on their feet, uncannily so. Xenath would probably kill him, but an angry voice in his head told him it would be worth it. His fingernails were already biting into each of his palms.

A bony hand stretched out and grabbed his arm, pulling him away from the stall. He turned quickly, prepared to strike whoever it was and looked into the face of the old woman he had seen a few minutes before.

She was hunched over, still clutching the bread she'd bought. She looked up at him, skin pale and rough like tree bark. So close now, Urdan could see the milky cataracts in her eyes and smell the acidic stench of urine from her clothes. When she spoke, he could see the black stains to her gums.

"Don't listen to him." She hissed, dragging them away to the other side of the square. "He cares only so long as he has a cock to wave at people." Her voice disintegrated into a wet hacking cough. Urdan dared a glance over his shoulder, feeling Xenath's eyes boring into him. "Turn yourself away!" The woman cackled at Xenath. "This conversation isn't for your ears. Find another sow to screw!" She pulled them out of his sight.

"My thanks." Urdan stumbled. "Did you hear? Do you know something?"

"It seems that Eroth is smiling today. A fortuitous omen I think." The woman continued, once she was sure that they could not be overheard.

Urden gave her a sideways look. It was strange to hear the drau goddess referred to in anything but a curse, let alone from an ancient looking human.

"So you're sister is lost?" The woman asked.

Urden nodded. "She left for the farm yesterday and did not come back." "The farm? That's a long walk to make these days. Why go all that way?" She looked at him thoughtfully.

Urdan sighed. "She wouldn't buy from Xenath." He could feel the worry and fear turn his anger to ice.

The woman patted his arm gently. "Don't fret. Eroth watches for strong women like Isola, she'll come back to you I have no doubt. Bartering with someone like that wont make it happen any faster."

Urdan swallowed and nodded. He wasn't particularly religious. They had been brought up by their human mother, who had spoken little on the subject and to his knowledge had never visited the shrine of Eroth accept at her death.

"I saw your sister a few times. She used to bring me apples in the winter when my leg got bad. I used to tell her that she should focus on herself. I've seen so many summers. I don't think that I would be too sad to not see another." Her eyes took on a wistful look. "She insisted nonetheless, wouldn't give up." She gave another wet laugh. "I saw your sister. She was coming back empty handed. She said the fields and the farm had been torched. I offered her what I had but she wouldn't take a crumb, said she would try elsewhere."

Urden felt the knot in his stomach tighten. "She seemed to think that she could find something outside of the village. The Dwentari, attack caravans headed for the city. I think she thought maybe there would still be something worth scavenging from the wreckage. Silly girl!"

The words refused to fully sink in. Urden felt like laughing. The very idea that Isola would even consider doing something so ridiculous it bordered on suicidal was absurd. It was almost a law by now. No one left the confines of the village.

*The rats have chewed into the larder again. I've tried to block the holes but they just keep on getting in.* Isola's voice haunted him again. *They've destroyed the dried beans.* Had she really been that desperate!

"I hoped that she thought better of it before she hit the road." The old woman was still talking. "But..." She paused, the implication obvious.

Urden braced himself against a wall as his legs turned to jelly. They had never been apart. Even when they had laid their mother to rest, when the cruel genetics of their father had lead them to do the same for their friends and family. They only had each other. If some- thing took Isola, if she was hurt or worse... "No." He shook his head. "No, I would know if she was gone. I'd know it in my heart."

"That's the spirit." The old woman smiled, her lips pulling rictus tight against her broken teeth. "Of course you would, but whatever has happened or not happened, has prevented your sister from returning."

Urden wasn't really listening. His head was buzzing. "I'm going after her." He whispered, unsure which of them he was trying to convince.

The old woman looked at him in shock. "You're what? No! You know what lurks beyond the palisade."

He had a fair idea. Since the Dwentari had bled across the plains, the world had been turned on it's head. Creatures from the dark places of the world had crawled and slithered from their hiding places and the wolves had grown bold, content to attack anything that moved. All of this was nothing in comparison to the damned Bone-men.

Harvesters. The Damned. They came when the battle had finished. Men and women, drau and human, who had weathered the torments their Dwentari oppressors had forced upon them. Twisted under the surgeons blade, rotting from the inside out, forever cursed to a state of permanent decomposition. They stood sentinel over battlefields, like scarecrows over fields of wheat. Fear, love, anger, these emotions had been scoured from their minds. Their teeth could chew through bone but in truth, they did not hunger. They yearned only to once again feel the warmth of skin and flesh long since lost to them. Wherever the Dwentari went, their ghoulish creations followed. Pulled on by their insatiable need and the scent of smoke and death.

Urden looked down at the old woman tugging frantically at his sleeve. His face was contorted with a worry only a grandparent could muster and for a second, he wondered where her family must have gone that she was left alone in the world under the weight of all those years.

"Don't go." She croaked. "But if you must, please be careful. Isola was a nice girl, if some tragic fate has befallen her, I doubt she'd have wanted her brother to go the same way." She tried to smile. "Eroth watch you." She whispered and limped away.

Urdan stared at the palisade gate. The night was coming in fast but the dirt road beyond was lit with the deep orange glow of the sun's last rays. Long fronds of course grass waved in the breeze, poppies bounced their blood red heads at him. Fingers beckoning him to come forward. Intoxicating.

Tentatively he took a step forward. Born and raised in the village, he'd had no need to go further than the nearest farm. Once, when he and Isola had been much younger, their childhood friends would defy their parents and dare each other to pick the furthest poppy from the grass beyond. Urdan had almost won once, before their mother had caught them. What a hiding she had given him that night, telling them terrible stories such that Isola had suffered nightmares for weeks of shifting shadows that reached for her with terrible claws, chittering through sharp, blackened teeth. In time these dreams had faded, but the lesson remained.

Urdan wiped his face on the back of his sleeve and stepped beyond the pallisade's perimeter. The sickening sweet smell of wet earth and dying flowers clawed at him. The grass hushed and whispered as he passed. He did not understand their language but he understood their meaning all the same. *Come little one, come and play in our garden.* He swallowed and closed his mind to their promises.

This time of year the weather was changeable. Winds from the mountains, chilled the air till frost formed on windows. Storms brought torrential rain that flooded the streets; but beyond the palisade, the air was more than just cold, it pulled the warmth from your very bones. Urdan fought not to shiver, rubbing his hands up and down along his arms and willing his blood to keep moving. He stopped for a second to watch the last single ray of the sun slide into darkness, bathing the world in a heavy twilight. Darkness. In the back of his head, his brain screamed at him to go back, warning him that only danger lay ahead. Showing him horrific images of what could lie beyond. In silence, he begged his mind to leave him be. Isola was lost out there. She was all he had left. He would not lose her.

So he walked. Slowly, hesitantly, almost crawling with every dragging footfall, he walked the dirt road till the scant lights of the village looked nought but fireflies and stars punctured the sky. There were no signposts, no clear demarcation for him to tell north from south or east from west. The dirt beneath his feet was lumpen and pitted. It crumbled and cracked with each footfall. In the dull light of the moon, the road seemed to shift and move. It felt as if he was walking along the back of some twisting serpent, any moment the monster would wake and strike at him even though he knew that such a thing was impossible. The road was no different to any other, he told himself but his mind would not agree. It twisted and convulsed, disorientating any attempt at direction. All the time, the grass rippled and whispered.

Urdan squinted ahead of him, trying to make out anything that might give him a clue, yet despite the moon, he could barely see the road ahead. A shiver ran down his spine. There was an oppressive sentience to it, as if the darkness was watching him, staring right back and daring him to take another step, observing his progress with mounting interest. He kept to the centre of the road. Who knew what dwelt beyond there, waiting for some unwary victim to snap up into it's clutches. No, it was better to keep your eyes firmly fixed ahead.

A sad moan echoed through the air, freezing his heart with it's unearthly note. Curiosity tempted him to look, to see who or what it was, but he would not. Hours seemed to pass and there had been no sign of Isola. In his heart Urdan began to despair.

Behind him a soft clicking caught his ears. Quickly, he turned, drawing the small knife from his pocket though he had little enough skill to use it adeptly. He swung in defence only to meet - nothing. Silence and darkness swirled before him like lovers. He turned, keeping the weapon tight in his grip, knowing better than to believe he was hearing things. Quietly, almost daring not to breath, he turned back the way he had been heading.

Urdan stopped when he came upon the crossroad. A tall staff of wood had been hammered into the ground. It's top was shattered but a moment's careful investigation found it's remains half buried at the foot of a gnarled tree. He pulled it free, the nailed planks coming away in his hand. Holding it up into the moonlight, Urdan tried to make out the name. Flecks of white paint still clung to the wood but time and weather had all but worn it smooth. He cursed under his breath and dropped it. As he reached out to pull another, he heard a scraping sound coming from his left, as if a stone were being dragged across cobbles.

A high pitched shriek issued from the road ahead. Urdan snapped to his feet, choosing a road at random and ran. He was being hunted, by what, he didn't dare to think. His feet hammered too loudly against the ground as he fled. One foot in front of the other, flying through the night. Despite the cold, sweat ran down his face at the dread of what might be following him. He reached out blindly, calling out Isola's name at the top of his lungs with every breath until, with a yell, he stumbled and fell sprawling face fist into the dirt. Pain blossomed across his face as he bit down into his lip. Blood coated his tongue.

Terrified of what he might find, he looked back to see what had tripped him. There in the middle of the road, a shoe lay on it's side. Urdan picked it up. It was a child's shoe. The white satin ribbons were frayed and torn. The sole worn through to the toe. The sound of slapping feet forced him to stand and turn, limping forwards, the shoe still clasped in his hand. A long moan made the air about him shudder. The hunters were coming.

He forced himself back into a run. In his peripheral vision he could see dark shapes darting out of the grass to join the chase. Dozens of them. Hunched and small, Urdan realized in horror that they might once have been children, now hideously changed. Sunken eyes stared out from pale emaciated flesh, sharp teeth chittered excitedly as they closed in on their prey.

Urdan screamed and sprinted, imagining their clawing hands reaching for him. He paused for breath at a rock, eyes darting wildly in desperation. He could not run forever and the urguls did not seem to tire. He must find somewhere to hide. As if at his bidding, the moon pushed past the broken sky, illuminating the husk of an overturned caravan. Half limping, he pushed on towards it.

The caravan lay on it's side, it's wooden frame cracked and splintered. The door to its interior swung on a single hinge and within, shadows clung to it. The still sane part of his mind told him to keep going, to find some other shelter, but the sounds from behind gave him little. It was this or painful death. Right now his only concern was survival and this seemed the best chance to be had.

They were gaining on him now. He could see them loping along the road, a gathering horde of hungry half dead creatures. Urdan looked back at the caravan. There was no choice now. He climbed up into the door frame, knowing that they would try to follow. They were hungry. Hopefully, they would kill him before dragging him out of his hole for the feast, but the way they looked, there was every chance they would simple begin while he was still alive.

The hinge screamed in protest as he lowered himself inside and pulled the door shut across the frame. Absolute darkness engulfed him. He reached out his hands, searching for obstacles. There was no sign of the caravan's cargo. Urdan reasoned that it had probably been looted months ago. He stumbled towards the back, further into the shadows. The air was damp and cold, like it had been submerged in a pool of brackish water and him with it. There was a stickiness to the touch that did not bare contemplation. A tiny shuttered window at the back looked out to the drivers seat. It's wicker mesh was torn and warped, the fine holes plastered with dirt and mud, but he could just about peer through it to the road ahead.

Outside, he could hear the urguls coming, their tiny feet moving with inhuman speed. He flattened himself to the back wall and held out the dagger, preparing to sell his life as dearly as possible - and yet the door did not open. He could hear their chittering outside but they would not enter. Cautiously, he turned back to the window and saw their grey, hairless bodies stalking around the perimeter, crouching defensively, heads raised as they scented the air. Urdan watched with horrified interest as they looked at each other, mewling under their breathe. Until, in unspoken agreement, they turned fleeing back into the grass from whence they had come. Within seconds they had disappeared, taking their cries of hunger with them. Silence returned, so thick it strangled the senses.

Gathering what remained of his sanity, Urdan pushed back the caravan door and stepped outside. He had no clue what had spooked the urguls to turn tail. He was hardly a threat, they could easily have dragged him out from his hiding place. While he might have been able to kill one or even two of them, their sheer number would have brought him down eventually. Urdan stumbled down the road. There was no where else to go but onward. If by some miracle he was still alive by dawn's light, he would look for some sign of the village but that hope was little more than a slim fantasy.

He had not got far when he found the remains of what once had been a camp, cloistered by a thicket of trees. His legs were dead and the thought of sleep was too good to pass up even here in the open. He stopped and looked at it warily. It was not far from the road, a thin, worn path lead to it, suggesting that it had been a frequent resting place for weary travellers. Perhaps Isola had found it too. Perhaps when it had become too dark to see where she was going she had decided to wait till morning. She could be there now, sleeping.

He approached. The moon cast strange shadows through the trees but there was still enough for him to make out a ring of bedrolls, rotting and covered in green moss. Urdan looked and felt his heart sink a little further. There was no sign of Isola.

Heavy-looking crates were stacked against the far side. His stomach grumbled at the thought of what they might contain. In better days these roads had been frequently travelled by merchants heading for the city. He picked his way across to them. Their lids had been torn away but Urdan reached right into the bottom, seeking scraps that might still remain. His fingers touched cold metal and clamped around it, bringing it out into the light. The object was a flensing knife. Urdan had seen the village tanner use one. It was marred with dried blood. He grimaced and threw it back into the box.

With the threat of immediate death passed, nausea and exhaustion clawed at him. He wanted more than anything, to sleep and let his body and mind recover. No, he thought. No, I cannot. He had to keep going. Isola was out there somewhere. Dead or alive he had to know. He had to bring her back. He licked his parched lips and pushed the dagger back into his pocket, stepping over a half-chewed bedroll. He had barely reached the edge of the camp when a halting voice came to him from the shadows between the two largest trees. "You're brave to have come so far in the dark." At first, Urdan was frozen to the spot in fright. He looked out to the road and almost made a dash back to the caravan, but the voice was not threatening and it only took a moment for him to recognise it. A bright burst of hope blossomed across him, banishing his exhaustion.

"Isola? Isola is it you?"

The silence was oppressive and absolute. Seconds dragged into minutes and Urdan began to believe he was hearing things. He turned away sadly and as he did so the sound of feet reached him. The footsteps were uneven, limping, as if one leg was being dragged across the ground. His heart beat a fraction faster. Had Isola hurt herself? Is that why she had not returned? Was she in too much pain to make the journey? Had the urghuls attacked her? The questions tumbled without halt as the strange scraping sound dragged closer. If Isola needed his help he was here for her now, he would bring her home. When the dawn came they would...

A pale shaft of moonlight wavered, casting awkward shadows as he turned. Even in the strange monochrome, he could make out the shape of a figure coming towards him. At first it was but another shadow among the shadows, but as it drew closer he could see details. The figure was tall and walked with a strange loping gate and pronounced hunch to it's back that spoke of a spine curved by age, labour, ill-luck or maybe all of the above. Urdan's heart fell. This was not his sister. The figure was swathed in a tattered, hooded cloak - a shroud of midnight. The hood fell low over it's face. Step by step it came closer, it's long fingers plucking at the air as if stroking an invisible harp. The closer it came the more Urdan wanted to run, yet he found his legs would not obey. The fingers reached out towards him in a mockery of welcome. Then the smell hit him, a wall of rot, decay, and disease that impacted with almost physical force. If he had eaten anything recently, he would have vomited. As it was he could still taste bile on the back of his tongue.

Who ever this poor creature was, it was not his sister. Nothing so loathsome could ever have been her - could it? Had something happened to her out here that she had chosen to stay away that this thing was responsible for? Urdan wouldn't have cared. If something had happened to her, they would find a way to change it or he would stay with her in this exile. There was no bond greater than siblings, it moved beyond simple flesh and blood.

He took a step towards the figure just as the creature reached up a hand and pulled back its hood. Urdan clamped his hand over his mouth but the squeak of his scream still escaped. The face beneath the shroud was so monstrous that no matter how much he begged, Urdan's mind would not stop staring at it. A grotesque mosaic of different parts, put together in the semblance of something that resembled a humanoid. One eye was milky with floating cataracts, while the other seemed to shine a vivid blue. The nose had a stitched seam that ran from bridge to tip and down the cupids bow where it met with feminine, painted lips that smudged across the chin. The mouth was open, lopsided much like the rest of it, and it sucked in grate lungfuls of air as if it was taking it's first breath of life. Between the lips, broken shards of tooth stuck up from swollen gums. In horror he realised that the teeth were so mismatched they could never have been the creature's own. Molars and canines looked like they had been rammed at odd angles into the fleshy, livid pink gum! Lank strands of greasy black hair hung lank over its shoulders and the ears, the ears were perhaps the most disturbing. One was tiny like an infants, quilt stitched to the side of the head. While the other barely remained, little more than a ragged stump.

It stopped a few feet from Urdan. Regarding him with an intelligence it had no right to have. The thing in front of him defied logic. By all accounts it should never have existed and yet here it stood. When it spoke it did so with vocal chords that cracked as the air entered them and as it opened its mouth with a stretch of old sinew, it let a out a single tuneless cry of utter desolation.

Urden felt his blood run cold. "You are a bone-man, a harvester!"

It was not a statement aimed at anyone but himself and yet the creature's lopsided smile belayed its understanding.

"I am remembered," it croaked in reply, taking another shuffling step.

Urden stumbled backwards, his brain was screaming at him to run but somehow he stood his ground. It's voice sounded both like it had no practice with its own vocal chords and there was a strange recognition in it's one good eye that was too familiar.

"Why do you skulk in the dark little one? Are the horrors of life so raw? Do you think so little of your soul to lose it so carelessly?"

Urdan swallowed and met the creature's gaze. "My sister is lost on the road. The Dwentari took everything we had. She was only looking for a loaf of bread or piece of meat. Our village is starving."

The bone-man looked at him, weighing his words carefully.

"You do not know hunger." It issued a soft child-like whimper. The creature's rouged lips stretched into a horrific smile. "What would you give to find her again."

Urdan studied the bone-man's long hair, stitched carefully to it's head, realising how similar in colour it was to Isola's. How a single matted braid was so like the one she had fashioned that morning.

"Anything," he whispered. "There is nothing I wouldn't give to see her again."

The bone-man nodded, the vertebrae cracking like broken wood.

Urdan feared that the head might come away altogether and yet a grim thought told him that the inconvenience of losing it's head would not necessarily hinder this creature.

"Come then little one. She waits for you in the lodge house can you not hear her calling?" It pointed through the trees with a hand that was little more than blackened bone gloved in skin.

They walked. Under what compulsion, Urden couldn't tell for every fibre of his psyche told him to run, run and run and not to look back. Yet here they were side by side, walking like old friends by some unspoken agreement. He could not hear the call this monster claimed to be his sister but he could feel it within. Something about the creature spoke of terrible truth.

Time ticked by soundless save for the steady scrape of their feet, till the trees thinned leaving only charred, torn stumps protruding from the earth. The ground had been churned to slick mud and a pervasive cloud of flies seemed to hug a few feet above the ground. Urdan tried his best to ignore the strange crunching sound as he pulled himself through it. He did his best not to look at the strange way the fallen trees looked more like half-buried cadavers in the trick of the moonlight. Amid the desolation, a single hut still stood. Rotten thatch was covered in heavy clumps of moss. Even from here, Urden could see no sign of life within.

He hesitated as the creature pushed wide the door and waited for him. "You do wish to see her, don't you?" It's head creaked alarmingly to one side and wobbled.

Urdan nodded.

"Come then." It's long finger coiled in on itself, beckoning him. "Come. We will talk of it."

"I..." He began, frantically thinking of an excuse to decline but his voice trailed away at the faint whisper of heavy breathing from within. Curiosity and terror waged a brief war inside his head before he stepped across the threshold.

The door banged shut, drowning him in darkness until his eyes adjusted. The stench of rot and old blood was so strong, Urdan fell to his knees retching. A bony hand reached for his shoulder, digging it's digits deep against his skin and pulling him up with a strength that did not seem possible. The Bone-man stood in the middle of utter chaos. Furniture had been torn to pieces, the homely trimmings of a simple life, scattered to the four points of the compass. Only a single table had survived, it's sturdy frame refusing to conform to its surroundings, flanked by a rickety looking chair.

"Where is she?" Urdan demanded, finally finding his voice.

The bone-man turned, amused by his sudden aggression. "I have met your sister. She was hungry and so very tired. She would not have lasted long without me."

Urdan choked a cry of worry.

"Would you like me to return her to you now?" The creature's fingers grated against the table, strips of dry flesh flensing from the ends.

"Yes!" Urdan gasped.

"Give me your hand." It rasped.

Despite the desperation he felt to see Isola alive and well, Urdan's arms felt like lead weights. Shaking to his core, he slowly offered his left hand.

Faster than he had expected, the Bone-man swung, the flash of mottled steel, glinted for a split second. Once. Twice. The third with a sickening crack of splintered bone.

Pain exploded across Urdan's arm. Bright spots in his vision threatened to push him off the edge of mortal sensation. The room quaked with a high-pitched shrieking and it took a moment for him to realise that the sound was his own scream tearing through his vocal chords. As the last of his breath ran out he slumped against the table. Blood bubbled from the end of the ragged stump, the splatter of it pattering against the floor like rain. He looked up through his own tears, to see the creature analysing it with all the care of a jeweller over a rare diamond. To Urdan's disgust, the creature grabbed its own wrist, snapping the brittle bone like a twig before ramming the bleeding hand onto it's own wrist with a meaty grinding sound.

What might have been a beatific smile passed over its seutered face. "So warm," it marvelled as the skin seemed to fuse to it's own tattered sinew. For a long moment all the bone-man did was admire it's new appendage.

Placing his remaining hand against the table to steady himself and pressing the stump against his body in a desperate attempt to staunch the bleeding, he staggered towards the creature. "Please..." he croaked, light-headed from the sudden loss of blood. He shuffled forward a few feet. "Isola..." The darkness came crashing in and mercifully, he lost consciousness.

Urdan opened his eyes wondering if he was dead. Was the bone-man even now picking over his corpse for fresh parts like some disgusting carrion eater? Slowly, sensation returned and with it pain. Pain on a level he had never entertained was possible. Water was raining down onto his face. *What fresh hell has this demon engineered.* His thoughts echoed painfully loud in his own skull.

It took him a while to realise that the water on his face was rain, the oddly soft sensation on his back was grass, and were those lights in the darkness? He tried to push himself up with his hands and screamed as pain shot through him blocking out all thought. Slowly, his mind cleared. He had gone to find Isola but... he looked at the stump of his left hand. The meat and skin was blackened and charred where the wound had been quarterized. Had it not been for that Urdan would have been prepared to put his encounter down to a terrible nightmare.

The sky above him was just beginning to tinge with grey at the edges. He stumbled to his feet, sliding against the damp grass. It was the early hours before dawn, still dark enough for ur-ghuls to see him as an easy snack. He wiped rain water from his face and squinted at the lights flickering in the dark - the village of Skelda was still sleeping.

"Your hand pleases me little one."

Urdan turned, unaware that the bone-man had been standing there the entire time. "Isola..." he began.

"She is well." The creature croaked. "At least in part, but if you wish to see her I will need more. I am old and her form pleases me."

Urdan felt his stomach turn as he realised what the creature was asking. A life for a life. An exchange. Murder.

"Urdan!"

The creature scuttled into the dark, away from the approaching lantern light bobbing towards them.

Xenath stopped short when he reached Urdan. The rain had plastered his hair to his skin and ran in long runnels down those pointed features.

"I saw you leave the village," he panted. "Eroth's fangs! Are you..." He caught sight of the stumpy remains of Urdan's left hand. "What in all the hells happened? Were you attacked?" He took a step back, raising the lantern high and squinting into the darkness then at him and took a step back.

It was utterly strange. Urdan had never seen Xenath like this. A mad laugh escaped his broken voice. "What's wrong Xenath, have you never seen a severed arm before. I walked into an old Dwentari trap. It took it clean off." The lie spilled amazingly freely from his lips.

Xenath looked at him suspiciously. "I collared that old bint and got her to tell me where you were headed. When I found out that you'd left town after Isola, I thought that you might need some help."

Urdan's face pulled into a slight sneer. "How heroic. Were you worried you might loose two more desperate customers." He looked towards the village. "You didn't come after me though did you? You've only just left. I'll wager that you saw me from the palisade, grabbed the nearest lantern and ran in to save the day. Were you hoping that I would return with Isola, the two of us so desperate and tired that I would agree to your latest terms? Or perhaps you thought that I would be at deaths door and easy to push off so you can do to Isola what you've always fantasised of." He could see Xenath's eyes narrow with anger and then before he could attempt to step back, Xenath punched Urdan across the jaw. He stumbled back into the mud.

"You mongrel piece of shit!" He spat as Urdan kneaded a split lip. "I should have shot you in the back as soon as you were alone but I figured that maybe you and I could make an arrangement. Maybe we could cut a deal to benefit the both of us. I let you live because I thought that if given time, you might come around but my patience grows thin." He paced. "You have any idea what a girl like that could go for? The Dwentari pay handsomely for drau women to take across the mountains." He stopped. "Not that you and your sister would fit that description but the Dwentari don't have the same distinguishing tastes." He stooped and grabbed Urdan's stump, illiciting a cry of pain. "I had a solid arrangement, now I'll be lucky if I make half that." He looked over the stump and grimaced. "An unfortunate flaw, but one they might overlook so long as your back is strong."

Urdan reached into his pocket with his right hand and found the small dagger. He gripped it tightly and rammed it to the hilt into Xenath's sternum. He withdrew it and rammed it again into the bastard's gut. Xenath gave a cry of pain and let go of Udan's stump, looking bewildered at the knife in his hand and then at the spreading darkness across his shirt. His face shifted from confusion of rage.

"You half-bred piece of scum!" he shouted, pressing a hand to the wound.

He stumbled forwards and before Urdan could stop himself, he had swiped in a wide arc clean past the drau slaver's throat.

His previous wounds forgotten, Xenath clasped his hands to his throat in a useless attempt to staunch the blood pouring over his fingers. Eyes wide in panic, he opened his mouth to speak but blood bubbled up and down the corners of his mouth.

Urdan looked at the blade slick with blood in horror. Stepping away as Xenath reached out to him, the crimson flow jetting from the cut artery and spattering Urdan's face. He stepped once to the right, then staggered to the left, before finally, falling face down in the mud motionless. Urdan stared at the body his heart pounding like a military drum inside his chest. Dropping the knife, he seized

Xenath's shoulders and started dragging him back away from the village. There was no going back now. The Bone-man was waiting and Urdan only had so many appendages.

Urdan dragged Xenath's cold corpse through the door of the hut not even gagging at the smell this time. Despite his fear of discovery, that he might not be able to find the hut a second time, he had pulled and carried the body through the early hours and into the morning to the Bone-man's door. Sweat ran down his back and his stump ached like the sharp beak of a raven was tapping at it.

The body dropped to the floor with the heavy thud of dead weight and Urdan slumped next to it. Exhaustion did not cover the level of tiredness he felt. He could barely muster the energy to look up at the unsettling creak of gristle and bone as the creature appraised them.

"Will this suffice? Tell me it is enough?" Urdan whimpered, nervously picking blood from beneath his fingernails.

The Bone-man pressed one of the fingers of it's new hand against Xenath's cheek and clicked it's cracked teeth in what Urdan could only assume was irritation.

"It is cold." The creature rasped. "The warmth is spent.

"Please, it is the best I could do!" Urdan begged desperately.

He watched in horror as the thick funeral cloak opened and half a dozen mismatched hands reached out towards the dead drau. "It will do." It's lips peeled back into a rictus grin as its arms seized Xenath, pulling him into an adjacent room while leaving a congealing smear Urdan cradled the stump of his left hand. The end was beginning to suppurate. *The pain will dull,* he told himself. It was worth it. Anything was worth it to have Isola returned to him. She was here. He would free her from this monster. His eyes drifted shut and cold dreamless sleep claimed him.

He did not know how long he had been unconscious only that the Bone-man was standing over him like some giant bird of prey. He tried to skoot back, banging his head against the table in his desire to be as far away from it as possible.

"It is done," the Bone-man stated and there was perhaps a note of tire in its voice.

Urdan looked around hopefully but saw no sign of Isola. He looked up at the creature's stitched face in disappointment.

"She needs to rest little one," it sighed like an indulgent parent and pulled it's cloak around itself tightly, as if gripped by a sudden cold. "Go home.

"How do I know you will keep to your word?" Urdan asked still groggy with sleep.

The Bone-man leaned in whispering, "because I have not yet harvested you."

Urdan's heart seemed to stop as the cadaverous face of the Bone-man hovered mere inches from his own. It's breath that of soil and decaying flesh. He swallowed and watched as the creature stood back to it's not inconsiderable height. It turned, loping unsteadily toward the back room. With it's back turned, he scrabbled towards the door, pausing with fleeting hope that Isola would join him.

"Leave!" The Bone-man rasped. It's voice echoing disturbingly loud, was enough to fray what remained of Urdan's senses and he fled.

The sun set the horizon aflame, turning the pools of standing water to blood as Urdan returned to the village. Xenath's disappearance had not gone unnoticed and like rats to corn, the village was descending upon what he had left behind, feasting on the bloated cadaver of his market stand. Soon they would descend on his home, bickering over the choicest trinkets.

Urden kept away, holding his arm inside his coat. Every noise made him jump, every shout made his heart tighten in his chest.

"Urden! Urden!"

He stood stock still as the shout of his name called across the street.

"Eroth's mercy! You are alive." The elderly woman, shuffled as quickly as she could to him. Her face squeezed into a smile as she showed her clutch of wrinkled apples and stale bread.

He recoiled as if she'd offered him his own bleeding heart, feeling the bile build once again in his mouth. Her smile was pulled so wide he could see the saliver building between her teeth. His head swam.

With a gnarled hand she held out an apple to him. "Take one." She insisted pressing it into his hand. "It is the least I can do."

His hand shook as she pushed his fingers closed around it and he felt the fruit give in his grip. Its thick juice squirted from where his fingers had broken the skin.

"What has happened to your hand?" She looked at him in alarm, squinting at the stump as if it were a trick of the eye.

He dropped the apple and shoved both deep into his pockets. "An accident," he managed, though he had barely enough breath to form the words. He was sweating, he could feel it rolling down the back of his neck and yet he shivered.

She reached out to touch him. "You are sick, Urdan. Eroth! You need to see a healer." Her voice creaked at the panic in her pitch.

"No!" He pushed her away, the look of shock on her face hitting him with the all the force of a blow to the head. He opened his mouth to apologise but found he had not the words. No one could cure him. The blood was still on his hands. He shut his eyes tight but he could still feel the blood running over them. He could feel the pop of ruptured organs beneath the blade in his grip. He opened his eyes again and stared in horror as the old woman stumbled backwards. A flower of crimson spread across her chest. She gave him one last look of confusion and regret before she fell to the ground and the rattle of her last breath faded to nothing.

Urdan dropped the blade, his eyes wide in horror. He had not meant to kill her. He just wanted to be left alone. He just wanted Isola back. She would understand, she would be able to fix him. He stooped and gathered the woman's things into his arms and turned toward home.

He arranged the feast upon the table and drew up a chair facing the door. The fingers of his remaining hand drummed against the wood as he stared, waiting for any shadows that might herald Isola's arrival. His nails scraped, shredding the mouldy wood into splinters that push up into his fingers but he did not feel it.

For how long he sat waiting, he did not know. Time had no meaning. He would not sleep, would not eat, would not relieve himself until Isola was returned. Suddenly his head jerked up. Beyond the door came the soft sound of stumbling foot falls.

Urdan stood unsteadily, watching the wood creak open and a hunched silhouette stumble past the threshold. He held out his hand, a smile cracking open the cut in his lip. "You were gone so long! I thought you were lost to me!"

The Bone-man had kept to his word. Isola half fell through the door. Tight stitching criss-crossed her face and arms, dark blood still slowly leaking from the needles mark. She looked at him expressionless. Pulling herself forward to the table.

Urdan's breath caught in his throat as he watched her staccato movements. Where was the sunshine of her laughter? Where was the light in her smile? This was not the sister that he had known. He shook the thoughts from his head. Of course she was not the same. How could she be after everything she had been through?

"I have made you a feast." He gestured to the table.

Isola looked at the food and back at him.

"It's alright if you aren't hungry." Urdan continued. "We can have it tomorrow." He stepped around the table slowly, not wishing to scare her. She watched him but no light of recognition glittered in her eyes. Tears, slipped from his crusted lashes as he felt the cold of her waxy skin. The Bone-man had been only fair. Urdan had delivered him a corpse and corpse had the Bone-man delivered. He cried out as her arms wrapped around him, pulling his tighter and tighter. *But that's alright*, he thought. Isola was here now, everything would be better. Nothing would ever take pull them apart.

The strength in Isola's arms squeezed him tight till her brother cried out in pain. Her mouth opened, the stitches tearing free at the corners. Her voice when it came, rasped and crackled like dry leaves in an empty grave. "So warm," she cooed quietly raking her nails down his arms. "So warm," she repeated over and over as Urdan began to scream.

# Drowned

"But die as lovers may - to die together so they may live together."
-Joseph Sheridan, Carmilla

The gull shrieked and wheeled, tossing against the wind like a child's kite. It screamed defiantly but the wind would not be tamed and in its rage, flung the bird against the stone column of the lighthouse with a sickening crack.

Maevis paid no heed to the drift of white-grey feathers in the air. Skirt hitched into a wide leather belt and wearing a pair of her husband's trousers beneath, she crouched over the floating corpse. She peeled back a strand of dark red hair, coarse with spray and salt. How had he died? She thought. Had he felt fear when he had realised that it would all be over? The drau warrior's face stared at her accusingly but they were miles from the nearest shrine, there would be no fine burial and she had little enough oil to maintain the lighthouse lantern. She looked back and flinched as the waves crashed against the rocks. The sea had taken this wretche's life and it would take the rest in time. It was coming for him even now.

Quickly, Maevis rifled through the pockets of his uniform. At least he could perform one last good act before the sea rose up to claim him. There was little enough on him. A handful of copper coins and a silver locket, the picture so water damaged that she could not tell who or what it had been off. With a sharp tug she snapped the chain from his neck and held it up. Perhaps it had once held the lock of hair from a sweetheart? She pocketed it and favoured him with one final look. What stories would you tell me? She wondered, but he was dead as the winter sun and he would never answer her. She shook her head and stood up, staring out to sea. In the mist and spray she fancied she saw the grey outline of a ship on the horizon. She blinked at it was gone.

There was little more warmth inside the lighthouse than there had been outside. Pictures she had once painted in better times, rattled against the wall in their frames. For a moment Maevis considered throwing another log into the small burner in the corner of the room.

She looked in the iron casket and with a sigh of disappointment, found it was empty. No surprise there. She reached out and picked up the kettle, steaming atop the tiny stove and poured a thin tea into a dubiously clean cup. It had been boiling for three days. She had topped up the water after each but there was little tea left within it. Still, the heat of it was nice. She didn't even mind that it burnt her tongue.

A large wooden cot hugged the far wall. It creaked a whimper as she sat on it, reaching back for the tatty quilt that lay crumpled at its foot. She wrapped it around her, inhaling deeply. It still smelt of him. Even after all this time, it still did. Beneath the sunken pillow, there lay a crumpled parchment. It had been folded and unfolded so many times that it was falling apart at the creases. Gingerly, she teased it open. The old creases cracked between her fingers to reveal elegant handwriting faded by touch.

This was her ritual. She dwelt nightly on this pain, torturing herself with the hope that by tomorrow's tide, he would return to her. This was the last letter he had sent. There had been no others. Ships had come and gone and still he had not returned to her. The truth in her heart told her he had been smothered by the waves. Tossed by the boiling waters; she could see him kicking desperately against the current, screaming for help that was miles away, swallowed by the darkness, thrashing, scrabbling, desperate for air...

She refolded the paper and rested her head on the pillow still clutching the letter in her hands. It could be worse. Maybe he had not met his end. Maybe he chose not to come to her like so many others she had heard of. Lovers, children, brothers, and sisters. The war had ripped the sanity from many that they no longer recognised the happy faces of their families. While for others, the horrors of battle were too near and they could not bear to return to the lives they once knew and left without a word.

She thought on this every night. Here on a narrow spur of land that reached out like a hag's finger from the port town of Darktide. Maevis glanced through the tiny window at the roiling water that hammered and crashed and kept its secrets shut. He was there, she knew it, still locked in the embrace of the waves. They called them The Mourners, these storms that moaned and shrieked across the shore like a banshee for it's mate. None sailed in such weather. Boats were lashed to the harbour and their owners filled the local dives to drink to oblivion, flirt with the local whores and try to block out the cold acres of the sea that groaned and muttered for their prey.

"Maevis!"

The a fist hammered at the door, shocking her to her senses and banishing these dark thoughts. In the miserable twilight, a face pressed against the window, one hand shielding it's face. She held back against the wall, pulling the quilt tighter.

"Maevis," he shouted again. "Are you in there?" With a barely audible groan, she pushed herself from the bed and unlocked the door, pulling it open just enough to see by.

"Kolvar," she said, pressing a smile to her face, while at the same time thinking: how can one get so fat on a diet of salt and air? He leaned against the stone lip of the door, pulling against his sealskin coat as the wind plucked and harried at him. Framed against a few dying rays, hair unkempt as it whipped about, he looked solid and unflappable. A family man and father to three young girls, he had not been called for the war effort. His business and shipyard, had made him too important to loose. She sniffed bitterly at the thought before feeling immediately ashamed for wishing such a thing.

"Eroth's fangs! Maevis, can't you see?" He tried to push into the small room.

"What?"

"This isn't good for you," he said. "Alone in this place. Haunting the beach like a ghost..." He reached out to touch her hand but she recoiled away from him. "He isn't coming back. Oren is dead."

Maevis felt her face twist into a frown. "You don't know that."

"He was a good one. We all loved him. His father taught me all I know of life. But you need to face the truth, no matter how painful it is. He's gone."

She looked passed him at the dirt and stone path that slithered towards the dark smudge of the town. For a moment she imagined she could see him there with his thick black hair and a wicked glint in his eyes

"The black waters of the Duma Sea are an unforgiving mistress," Kolvar prompted.

"I know," she admitted quietly. "But how can I let him go when there is no body - no final goodbye."

"Mae..."

"He should be there," she gestured to a heavy set seat in the corner of the room. "Not lost, afraid, and alone. You don't understand. He will come back to me, one way or another. The sea will give him up and when it does, I'll be waiting for him," she continued, the fervor creeping into her voice.

Kolvar gave an exasperated sigh. "You're barely living out here," he pointed at the dying embers in the stove and the empty scuttle. "At least come back with me, stay in the town. I've room for you and the girls can share. Just till Spring when the storms pass," he pleaded.

Maevis simply looked at him sadly.

"You're too soft for the north. I've always said your family should have found you a nice suitor down south but you and Oren were more wrapped up in each other than any I've seen." He tried to smile. "I'm known in town, Maevis. I've got to try with you. People are beginning to talk. Sympathy will only go so far and I think you've got as much as you're going to get."

"I don't care about their sympathy," she snapped. "They can think what they like."

He dismissed her anger with a wave and turned back towards the town, murmuring in a low, uncertain voice: "These storms are the worst they've ever been, take it from me. Don't stay out here much longer, please. My door is always open."

Before she slept that night, she closed her eyes and recited the names of those who had left with him, as she did every night: Tannatar Elquen, Jhaan Shanala, Shael Virnelis, Morthil Veth-Soris... the motion of her lips sparking the memory of a forgotten soul. As she recited them she wondered if those names now sat in Eroth's Court, raised resplendent at the heroes feast. Oren was no coward, his place was affirmed of that she was certain.

When the wind died down, she snuffed the candles. The lights of Darktide cast strange shapes outside the window. The town's low dwellings, clustered like barnacles to the cliff edge. Outside, the wind gave a final clatter against the totems nailed to the door frame. Shells and fish-bones, scrimshawed with their names to keep the greedy sea at bay. The sea hushed and rattled against the rocks. She lay back in the darkness listening to that endless song. Once, many years ago, Oren had serenaded her to the backing of that sound. She suppressed a giggle at the memory of that utterly tuneless melody. Now there were only long, empty evenings ahead of her; the snap and pop of embers in the burner, and the repetitive squeak of the lamp high above her as it rotated on its mechanism. Home, she thought. It was a bitter image.

As sleep gently eased her eyelids closed, she heard it: a noise in the dark. Eyes wide, she clutched at the quilt, pulling it up to her chin. Silence. Nothing but the sea. Her fingers fiddled with the fraying seam, teasing the thread free until, after a long, sour moment, it came again - low, strangled, and burbling through the night. Her stomach knotted and she reached for the candlestick, striking it alight once more.

"Kolvar?"

A skittering of shale and stone. Sea birds, she thought, it's just a gull or two looking for a place to shelter, or maybe one of the small whales, separated from its pod, beached by the storm and waiting to die. *Eroth, something was out there!*

A twisted scream lanced through the night and before Maevis had time to think about what she was doing, she had thrown on a heavy cloak, hurried across the room, and flung wide the door, her breath coming in rapid gasps as she stared into the night. The scream came again, agonised, pain-filled, clawing at her with invisible hands.

She drew up the hood and stepped into the darkness. The sound had drifted down to a tortured, animalistic wail. Maevis swallowed and steeled her nerves. It took everything she had to make her way back to the rock pools, a surprising well of courage that she'd thought had been lost the day they had come to take Oren away. If something was hurt out there, if it was still grasping to life, then surely the sea had spat it out for a reason. It was not meant to die here.

The shale shore spread out before her, an ever expanding carpet of stone shards lit only by the poor light of an ill moon. Every now and then it reflected off a breaking wave, a shimmering that held a malevolent magic to it, and something else... a dark shape that pulsed and shivered and fell with the tide. She stared at it, part of her willing it to hit the beach and when it did, she cautiously crossed the stones towards it: towards the stunted, lumpen shape that floundered against the waves. Wounded and gasping for breath, it croaked a single, mangled word: "Help!"

Dawn came though the sun had yet to know it. "Eat." She said slowly, holding a bowl of thin soup and held up the spoon. It bubbled from it's lips and down it's chin. She sighed and reached for the cloth, dabbing gently, still afraid that it might try and bite her. She sat back. Her bones were heavy with exhaustion. She had pulled the creature from the sea, amazed that it had survived the storm, and dragged it to the lighthouse. What divine grace had saved it, she knew not but the sea had seen fit to send it to her and who was she to argue.

Maevis stared at it, watching the shallow rise and fall of its breathing. Matted black hair sprouted from it's jaw and more even thicker, from it's head. Though short, it was muscled like an ox and so it had turned out, was just as stubborn. She had never seen a Dwentari before. Their like were told only in horror stories from those who had seen the fighting to the south and returned with enough wit to tell of it. Yet, this was not what she had expected. So small and more beast looking than man. It stared back at her with almost absurdly large, blue eyes. Was it as scared of her as she was of it?

She placed the bowl on the side and brought up a clay cup of tepid water. "Drink." She offered.

It did not respond.

She tipped the cup to her mouth and took a sip. "Drink." She repeated.

It snarled something harsh and cursed at her.

She shook her head in exasperation.

It looked at her, blinking like a newborn. Spit drooled from the side of it's mouth, and it emitted a deep moan that made her think of a calling seal. At other times, it's eyes seemed to focus on her like a steel trap, a look of bitterness and hatred wrapped across it's face.

"I'm trying to help you." She said softly. "Do you have a name?" She waited. "Family?" She asked when only silence came. "Children?" She continued, making the action of a rocking baby.

It groaned and rolled away. Eventually, by the laboured rise and fall of it's chest, she realised it had fallen asleep.

Maevis started to clear the bowl and cup away. Her first thought when she had gone out to it, was that somehow the sea had heard her call and returned her husband to her, but then the waves had turned it over. It had worn nothing but rags and broken scraps of what might once have been armour, tarnished with salt. It had gurgled and wretched as it clawed desperately for land, drawn to her like a moth to the flame. It had taken her an hour to haul it from the tide's grip and all the time wondering, what had caused it to be almost swallowed by the sea and flung towards the lonely shore. What strange twist of fate had brought it so far north. She crept from its side and made herself a small next from old blankets, on the floor. A cold wind pressed against the lighthouse, creeping under the door. She tried to rest, tried to ignore the gagging stench of wet dog that exuded from the thing that was sleeping in her bed, until the exhaustion finally took her.

"Maevis?" The door rocked as a heavy fist hammered against it. Kolvar's voice once again, called from the other side. The melancholic light of mid-morning fell through a chink in the curtain. She groaned and unravelled herself from the cocoon she had created. For a moment, she gazed at the Dwentari. Its savage, barbarian face was fixed firmly on the door.

The knocking wrapped again. "Maevis? Are you still asleep?"

She cursed under her breath and threw a blanket over the creature, motioning for it to be quiet. Straightening herself out, she opened the door.

Kolvar was not alone. A stooped and wrinkled individual stood to his side. Akaida was the oldest Drau she had ever known. Leaning against the wall of the lighthouse like an animated corpse, she fixed Maevis with a pair of steely silver eyes that age had not tempered. As soon as Maevis opened the door, she pushed her way inside.

"What do you think you are doing?" She protested. "You can't just burst into my home like this?"

"And why not?" Akaida's voice was like tortured metal. "With your lover lost, I doubt that there's much to offend me." She limped into the room, looking it over. Her eyes alighted on the pile of old blankets on the floor and the unwashed kitchenware on the hob.

Kolvar looked at her apologetically. "I'm sorry Maevis, but this really has gone on for too long." He forced a smile. "Just try it. Akaida says she can take you on at the tap house and the pay isn't terrible. You might even find you like it - you know, take your mind off things."

"But..." Maevis began.

"Think you're too good for it?" Akaida grumbled as she trundled about the room, picking up the blankets on the floor and dumping them in a net hammock on the wall before peering into the now cold pot of soup. "I know your love's gone." She looked back, not unkindly. "It was the same when I lost mine. We all get claimed sooner or later but for now, life continues and so should you." She turned to head for the door and stopped. Before Maevis could stop her she picked up one of the broken armour pieces off the floor. She turned it over in her hands and studying them in the faint light.

"Been scavenging again have you?"

"What of it?" She replied defensively.

Akaida shrugged. "Some young one said he found tracks. Said something had pulled itself from the sea."

"Like what?" She asked, trying to sound calm.

Akaida shook her head. "Wouldn't know, the tide swept it clean." She gave her a long, hard look.

Maevis kept her face blank, feeling her heart thunder in her chest.

"Well," She said finally. "I expect you at the Sea Call at midday. There's floors to sweep and dry throats to quench." Her nose wrinkled. "For the love of Eroth, Maevis! Open a window or something, it reeks of death in here." She turned and pushed past Kolvar who gave her one last apologetic look before leaving, closing the door behind them.

Maevis waited till the sound of the feet on the rough gravel faded against the rumble of the sea. She gasped for breath and wiped the sweat from her forehead. She rushed to the bed and pulled back the blanket. The Dwentari stared at her and said nothing.

"You're safe." She spoke, unconvinced that it understood any more Rhegarsi then she did of whatever tongue it spoke with. "I won't let them hurt you." She carried on unpeturbed. It looked at her but somewhere in those blue eyes, she was sure that it was grateful.

Maevis threw herself into local life like she hadn't done in years. She smiled at the older Drau coming in from the ship yard, worn and tired. She brushed down the floors, and ferried food from table to table. All the time she was aware of their wary stares. Drau she had known since childhood didn't talk to her, while others whispered as soon as she had turned her back. It was as if she was contagious, like her loss was an ailment that nobody would risk to catch.

"Don't worry about it." Kolvar smiled, patting her hand when he visited at day's end. "Most of them have nothing to talk about and any scandal would rile them up."

"What scandal?" She asked.

Kolvar laughed as he took the drink she offered him. "Some have been saying that you have a new lover."

"What?!" Maevis started, hushing herself as few heads turned.

"Wouldn't care if you had." Kolvar continued. "You're still a young, good-looking girl. No need for you to live out your days in solitude like Akaida if you don't want to, and it's none of my business either way."

She opened her mouth to reply as a voice from the bar yelled for her attention. Kolvar shooed her away. "It's just a bit of gossip. Give it a day and they'll find other things to whisper about."

By the time she finished that evening, her muscles were sore but in a good way. It had been so long since she had felt of real use, she yawned. She would sleep well, and if she dreamed, she knew that Oren would visit her. He wasn't far now. All the lost things were coming home.

Kolvar walked her back, holding the lantern between them. "So, do you think you will take Akaida up on her offer? Will you be back tomorrow?"

Maevis started, she'd been unaware that he'd been talking to her all this time. "I'll think about it tonight." She rushed. "The lighthouse needs a tidy and..."

"I understand." He cut her off. "No need to make excuses. You need to move on with your life."

They stopped as they reached the lighthouse door.

"You know, we could hold a funeral for Oren up on the cliff." He added, tentatively.

"But there's no body." Maevis stated.

"Well, I don't see why it should be a problem. I'm no zealot but I'm sure Eroth knows. None of us have ever been to her court but I am sure that he's there - a brave young soldier like that. How could he not be?"

The wind moaned, kicking up the surf on the sea. "Akaida said someone found tracks this morning." Maevis changed the subject.

Kolvar gave an exaggerated shrug. "I wouldn't worry about that. It's nothing."

"Maybe, a whale beached further down the headland." She offered.

He shook his head. "Nothing so likely." He smiled. "I wouldn't pay any heed to it. A few things were found washed up on the beach but they could have been dredge up from miles down the coast. A few of the guard will come down from the castle to patrol just in case. Goodnight Maevis." He turned and headed back up the path towards the town.

Maevis watched as the twinkle of the lantern shimmered till it was nothing more than the size of a glow bug. She put her hand on the door and was surprised by the sudden give. Pushing open the threshold, she knew instantly something was wrong. Even in the pale moonlight, she could see flecks of what might have been blood on the step of the door.

Inside, the room had been turned upside down. Pans lay dented and scattered to the compass points, the door of the stove had been pulled from it's hinges, straw from the mattress lay scattered across every surface. She stopped, listening intently but all she could hear was the music of the sea. She turned and looked frantically up the path towards the town. Quickly, she ran into the lighthouse, seized an old lantern, lit it, and dashed back out to the night.

She found it. Lying by the roadside, slumped in a gulley, partly filled with foetid water. It's eyes turned to her as it panted in pain.

"What in Eroth's name did you think you were doing!" She almost yelled at it, keenly aware that if Kolvar had but looked in the wrong direction on their return, he would have seen it. "You could have been found!"

It scrabbled to move and moaned, clasping it's side.

"I know." She soothed. "But you aren't strong enough yet. Come on, let me get you back to the lighthouse." Maevis reached down, trying to pull it up with one arm while the other clutched the lantern. Suddenly, she head the tinny tread of metal and heavy feet. She looked up in horror as the moonlight reflected off two armoured figures making their way up the path. Without thinking, she leaped into the gulley and hunkered down beside it. Over the lip she could sea two guards, old salts, armed with barbed blades and a rusty lamp. One spun a sword with a lopsided grin.

"A few swings of this and I'll be feeding it to Eroth piecemeal." He boasted.

The other laughed and passed him a flask. "Let me tell you, they're tougher than they look. You'll be hacking for a good while."

The patrol walked on, still laughing.

When they had passed, Maevis breathed. She looked down and realised that she was holding it's hand. It looked at her and gasped its only second word: "Why?"

She looked at it in surprise at herself more than the suddenness of the question. "Because..." She began, her mind drifting back to the way it had looked at her as she'd pulled it from the sea. "Because who else will help you!"

She helped it back to the lighthouse, scooping enough straw back into the mattress, to ease it into bed. As it rested, she picked her way through the chaos, righting the room to something that resembled normality. She fond an old ball of yarn and began darning a pair of woollen tights, while the soup reheated on the last embers of the heat from the stove. Twice she heard the clatter of armoured feet pass the door, each time it made her hold her breath until it had passed.

As midnight came, she looked over at it lying in the bed watching her. She smiled. "You know, this reminds me of when Oren was here." She watched it's confusion. "We were bound together." She explained. "He used to watch me. Just while away the hours, content because the other was there." She put down the darning and edged towards the window, peering past the curtain.

The town glinted like a handful of starlight thrown on the coast. All was perfectly quiet until... she blinked, for a moment she thought she had seen a figure on the edge of the path but when she looked again it was gone. She listened. There was no sound of footsteps or the clatter of the patrol, only the steady swell of the sea. *Perhaps they have given up?* She looked at the Dwentari. So long as there were others looking for it, it couldn't stay here. She considered her options, though she was loath to let it loose for the company it had provided. Perhaps she should let it free on the coast. "He's dead."

The rasping noise of it, made her jump. She blinked in surprise before the heavy weight of Oren clamped back firmly onto her heart. "I know," she whispered. "I didn't want to believe it, but if the sea brought you back, it would have returned him to me also." She wiped a tear from her cheek and tried to smile. "Oren was brave and fearless. Eroth will have accepted him, rights or no."

It looked at her in confusion and slowly closed it's eyes. She smiled and gently arranged the covers, crawling beneath them herself. It wasn't really so bad - the smell. It just took time to get used to it, like it's owner. The pair of them, such a strange couple and yet so similar, both alone and lost where the shore met the sea.

She listened to it's breathing, laboured but easing. Evidently, their hardy reputation was warranted. She smiled and closed her eyes, imagining that it was the sound of Oren's snores she could hear. Sleep gently wove it's arms around her, muffling the noises of the night with it's disarming embrace.

She awoke with a gasp, the sound of voices echoed from outside and the clatter of armoured feet. There was a crash against the door - harsh shouts. She screamed as the glass of the window beside them shattered.

The Dwentari was awake. *How long had it been watching her?* It snatched up a table knife from the pile of unwashed crockery and looked at the door snarling like a feral beast.

"Maevis! Maevis, let us in, or we'll burn you out!" The smell of smoke began to curl around the room. "We know you're hiding it!"

"Leave us alone!" Maevis screamed, glancing about for a way out. *How did they know?* She had been so careful. *Akaida.* The thought solidified in her head like a shard of ice. *Akaida had known something the second she had picked up that lump of metal.* Her brain buzzed angrily. *How? She must have seen it before. She recognised it.*

The top panel burst from her door and blades hacked their way through, splintering the wood.

She screamed. "Leave me be!"

The door whined on it's hinges and came away. Kolvar stepped through. "You've been seen consorting with that thing." His eyes drifted towards the creature with a look of pure, undiluted hatred. "We've known for a while that someone was ferrying the bastards inland. Eroth knows, you were the last person I thought could stoop to such depths."

"It was drowning," she pleaded. "I couldn't let it die. Not like Oren."

Kolvar looked at her in disgust. "Kill it," he growled as others began to press into the confined quarters of the lighthouse room.

The Dwentari grunted something in its strange guttural tongue and though she did not understand it, she felt it's intention. There seemed to be such fury in it just then and even weakened as it was, she feared it was more than a match for half the Drau out there.

Flames began to lick up the building, catching the curtains through the window.

"This way." She grabbed it's hand and dragged it up the stairs of the lighthouse. She could hear Kolvar calling out for her behind them as they climbed around and around, till confronted with the light of day at the apex. They both stared at the trapdoor even as they heard the yells of those coming for them.

"Don't hurt them," she said to it, taking its hand in hers.

The trapdoor burst open. She turned and fumbled with latch of the lantern-house windows. Far below the high tide lapped at the stone base of the lighthouse. She swung the crystalline glass wide enough to climb through just as a pair of rough hands clasped her shoulders. Kolvar pulled her back towards the smoke filled stairs.

"Kolvar, please..." she begged. "Just let it go."

"Get out of my way!" he barked at her. The point of a blade, flashed silver then red. She watched as Kolvar gripped his throat in terror as the life jettisoned out of him in bright red bursts.

The Dwentari stood beside her as Kolvar toppled back though the hatch into the smoke and flames. She looked at it in horror. "What have I done?" she whispered. Gone, she thought. All of it. My whole life. Tears welled and slid down her face. Oren, I'm sorry.

More voices, angrier than Kolvar's, echoed from beneath them accompanied by the crackled of burning wood.

"Go!" it growled at her.

She stared at the window and eased herself out onto the ledge beyond while the Dwentari covered her from behind. She thought again of Kolvar and shivered. Did she dare disobey this creature? Would they forgive her if she did? A loud bang made her heart leap into her mouth and she fell.

For a few tantalizing seconds, Maevis was weightless. Then the sea came rising up to meet her, rushing to pluck her from the sky. She crashed into the water and tumbled beneath the waves. The current dragged her down as she kicked out, her clothes wrapping around her, making her feel a hundred times heavier than she actually was. Over and over it tossed her, bubbles of air bursting from her mouth as her leg scraped against the sharp rocks beneath.

The surface was tantalizingly close. Through it's warped mirror she could see the lighthouse above, streaming with flames. Dozens of dark shapes clustered on the cliff edge. They threw something into the water, though she couldn't see what it was, the tide dragging her further and further away.

Spots of darkness danced at the edges of her vision and she fell back into the currents embrace, utterly spent. The headland blurred under the constant motion of the water and far flung brittle shore. I'm coming *Oren. I am done with this.*

She felt herself pulled along, turning like a leaf in the breeze, towards the black oblivion. Then it was cold, so cold it hurt. Some dim, smothered part of her reached out, seeking that peaceful resting place. That hall of stone and glass, where a true mother's love was waiting for her lost child, but the fairytale did not come and she was fluttering away into nothing, like the cresting foam, untethered from the waves, floating on a violent tide.

They found her, sprawled across the shale shore. Her clothes and legs were torn to ribbons. "An omen," they said. "Even the sea would not accept her." They laid her with Kolvar's body in the bottom of the tap house till it could be decided what should be done. Akaida had called a meeting. It would be early. There were dark sails on the horizon.

# Old Man Splinter

"*I have lost the faculty to enjoy their destruction, and I am too idle to destroy for nothing.*"
-Emily Bronte, Wuthering Heights

"Filthy trees," Zhegra grumbled. "They offend me, Bhegrin." The Dwentari stroked the steed's scaled neck as she spoke. The lizard-beast hissed, snapping its jaws to reveal rows of needle sharp fangs in what might have been agreement. It raked a clawed paw across the ground, gouging deep groves in the hard earth. Sithaxi beasts despised the cold. Zhegra leaned forwards in her fur-strewn saddle as the remains of her small retinue felled another tree. It toppled with a bone shaking groan, striking the ground with a crash.

"Bring them all down. Shatter them. Leave nothing but stumps," Zhegra instructed. "If I do not find a way through this accursed woods by nightfall, one of you will bleed for it."

Blades and cleavers bit into thick stumps and smashed against roots and branches, the ground littered with broken shards of wood and shattered trees. They worked diligently, heaving, sweating, as they sought to clear a path through the knot of briar and branch that still yet resisted them.

They had been separated from the main force for days now. Zhegra wondered if her alter-ego Rhagrasan had seized the opportunity of her absence and wormed his way to the right hand of her commander yet. It had crossed her mind that this might yet be an attempt to remove her permanently. But no. The Drau had simply been more tenacious than expected. They had mustered in defence of their city in far greater numbers than had been predicted and the Dwentari had been forced to withdraw. She turned aside and spat the bile from her throat. Not a defeat. A tactical retreat. Now they knew the numbers ahead, next time, they would shatter them like the trunks of these trees.

"Set a fire," she called, turning the Sithaxi about the better survey the destruction. "We will burn our way back to our lines if we must. I will burn every acre. Once we are regrouped with our kin we will break our pursuers upon an iron shield and make even this wild place fit for civilised people."

Zhegra lifted Razortooth and felt the weight of the blessed runes carved into the bone of the haft wrought to its steel blade. It pulled at her soul, tiny barbs stitched into the flesh of her hand. The sharp pain of it a pleasing sensation. It left welts in her flesh where she clutched it. Zhegra believed that the weapon had a life of its own, desirous of nothing save to destroy the enemies of The Silver Fortress. It had been a gift - a token of appreciation from the Iron Lord himself, whose ash plains she had defended against the wretched revolutionaries and their depredations. Shield-maiden Zhegra of Kherdrom he had named her.

She thought of that and smiled, sitting regal in her saddle, clad in the tattered finery of her station. The Iron Lord had seemed sad at her leaving. But, she was a warrior first and the call of war pulsed in her blood as surely as her own heartbeat. The axe had been borne by many champions all the way back to the first Dwentari warlords that had placed stone and steel to the land. Its blade was pitted by the innumerable battles it had seen, touched by the warlocks of the fire lands and imbued with the weird of their magics. It was an axe worthy of all the destructive potential of the name Razortooth. Like her, it was a sign of the Iron Lord's favour.

And that favour was why she, above any others, would be the one to crack the rich lands of the Draurhegar. For it required speed of limb and the bloody will to breach the tricks and wiry feats of the Drau themselves. Zhegra raised her axe and bellowed encouragement as another tree slammed against the ground. Around her, her retinue did the same, calling out to their brothers and sisters in support or mockery as they deemed fit. Like Zhegra, they were loyal to the Iron Lord. Theirs was a sacred duty. The will of their mightiest made manifest.

The Sithaxi screeched and hissed, tearing the ground with its claws as the ground began to clear. Their voices ebbed, seeing the remaining trees beginning to thin and sway, as if caught in a breeze. The chatter died as every ear strained to hear the sound, in case it was the sign they had been seeking.

It was a soft thing. Like loose leaves across bare fields. Zhegra tightened her grip on the axe. Soft sounds were dangerous. Experience had taught her that they too often were the precursor to a Drau attack. The Sithaxi stirred restlessly. The lizard-beast snapping and she reached down, calming it with a hand on its sagging neck. "Easy," she murmured. Far above, in the high canopy, branches rustled and then fell silent.

Zhegra looked around, the tattoos at the corners of her eyes twitching. She feared no mortal enemy, but the 'Dark Ones', the Drau's specialized warriors, they gave her pause. It felt as if the clearing was alive with a thousand eyes, watching, waiting.

She'd fought the assassins before, they had come for the camp and been thrown back into the night with blade and bale-fire. Nevertheless, it was unnerving and she did not possess the numbers to throw them back with any surety. They came so suddenly, and with such ferocity that even a moments inattention could mean the difference between life and death.

"Where are you," she muttered. "I can feel you, watching. Are you afraid little Drau? Do you fear the sting of my blade?" She hefted her axe, waiting. Nothing answered the challenge.

But they would. This realm, the northern lands entire, was aware of the coming of the Dwentari. She had to admit, they were not a subtle people. The witch-king of the Drau had been driven to wrath, and sent his best servants to harry them into the wild. Now shadows shook the encampment at Hag's Rise and many others. What had been an unstoppable slaughter had petered to murderous skirmishes that were lost as often as they were won. Secretly, Zhegra couldn't be more pleased. It had been decades since she had felt any real challenge.

The sound faded, as quickly as it had come. As if paled, a new more welcome noise replaced it. The guttural tongue of her own kind and the whine of hounds. The beasts loped into view, bounding over fallen trees with long-limbed grace. They were hairless and covered in scars, their blunt and squashed faces streaming drool. They had bulging eyes and long dark tongues that lolled as they sprang at Zhegra in greeting. Her sithaxi hissed and spat at them, unappreciative of their attention. It was a proud creature. Zhegra laughed and pushed an over-affectionate hound from her saddle.

"Hail, and well met, my lady," a rasping voice said. A broad figure, swaddled in grimy furs and streaked armour stepped out of the trees, on arm bandaged and strapped uselessly to his chest. His other hand held a long and cruel looking whip.

"Hail, and well met, hound master. Good-hunting then?" Zhegra asked.

The hound-master was one of many but had fought beside her before and for longer than many others. Though his years made him frail and slow, the hound-master was strong in the ways of war, and as loyal as one of his four-legged beasts that trotted beside him. Zhegra had dispatched him to forge ahead, his hounds hampered not by the press of the trees like they were.

"Aye, my lady," he replied and whistled.

A pair of hounds cam dragging their prey excitedly across the ground and dropping it at his feet. The hound-master planted a foot on its back. He caught hold of a tuft of smoke grey hair and bent its sharp features up for his lady's inspection. The Drau was dead, or not far from it. Blood leaked from the mauled tatters of flesh across its face and dribbled to the ground where the hound-master deposited it.

"Can it speak?"

He made a face. "Do they ever? They would rather cut out their own tongues than give sound to our words. This one was no more capable of conversation than my hounds," he replied and let the head sag. I thumped into the soil. The Drau shivered, leaking its body fluids across the ground. They were such fragile things for being so deadly.

"Where there is one, there are others," Zhegra said and watched her companion nod.

"Aye," he agreed, giving a gap-toothed smile. "Sure as my heart beats, my lady. We'll find the others."

"It is not us finding them that concerns me, it is them finding us," she replied sternly. "This one," she pointed at the fine-fitting, black attire of the bleeding victim. "This one stalks shadows like a spectre."

"We will find them, my lady. Your axe will fall and they will learn to fear the dark again." His voice was determined repeating the omens that had been spoken by the oracle on their departure.

Zhegra shifted in her saddle. She did not let on the unease she felt about the blind oracle of the Silver Fortress. It was said they could read the skeins of fate. She remembered the hag's voice in that instant, the way that she had looked at her with those white, crusted eyes. *There had been something there,* she thought. *Some trace of what? Sadness? What had she seen?* She pushed the thought aside and ran a thumb along the edge of Razortooth, kissing the skin.

Pain brought clarity. Clarity was a Dwentari's greatest weapon. To see the world as it was, stripped bare of the tattered mask of desire, leaving only beautiful facts and revealed resource. There was comfort in that, and joy in the thought of fresh prospects. Zhegra glanced about the remains of her retinue. She knew their names and the victories they claimed, they were like siblings to her - some were heroes in their own right, like brawny Bhegrin, who had once wrestled a Fomorian for three days in the mines of Nogvorod. She liked him. Perhaps, if this accursed place came to an end, she would rut with him later and test his strength against her own.

Pride swept through her, as, one and all, they met her gaze, She raised Razortooth. "For the Iron Lord and the Silver Fortress," he said. Barbed swords and serrated axes rose in salute. All around the clearing, the Dwentari readied themselves to march.

She looked at the hound-master. "We go quietly from here, like the last embers on summer's eve. Lead the way. Take us out of here."

The hound-master nodded and turned, chivvying his dogs into motion. The beast barked with pleasure and loped away. Her Sithaxi trotted in their wake.

Zhegra thought she felt Razortooth squirm in her grip. The axe was eager. It knew it had business ahead. The Drau might be hunting them, but when they mustered with the rest of her force, the tables would be turned. She looked down at the dying Drau as she rode past. "Toss that creature on the fire. I have a land to tame."

The Outcast slept.

It's addled thoughts surged up and down into the darkness at the root of it, crashing and cascading over the rocks of broken memories. There was only the rush and roar of them in its mind, drowning out all else save the reaping wind.

The war-wind.

Old man Splinter couldn't hear anything over the shriek of it save his own voice, and that only dimly. It had always been that way, for as long as he could remember, which was not as long as he would have liked. His mind faded with the season, reason growing bare like wind stripped branches. In the season of new sunlight, he could hear the trees whispering to one another as they stretched towards the sun. They did not speak to him, but he could hear them nonetheless.

Now, at this moment, the Outcast heard it all, but it did not stir. He refused to stir. He was intent on sleeping through the fathomless ages. Yet, he could hear the weeping trees as their bark split and the sap spilled. The important roaring of the stones as there surfaces were left seeping and scarred. Not all wept, not all roared, some sang. Desperately, defiantly, they sang.

He heard it all, but he did not stir. He refused to stir. He would sleep. He would sleep until these destructive creatures were nothing, and then her would continue to sleep until the world unwound. Better to sleep, better to ignore.

*What do you fear, Old Man Splinter?*

The voice was soft, at first. Like the sound of newly sprouting leaves in a breeze. A gentle sound, and it placidity irritated him, though he could not say why.

*Awaken, stir your roots and stretch your limbs. Awaken old man.*

The voice grew stronger and the Outcast shivered in his sleep. The sound of rain striking the canopy, a hint of distant thunder. There was pleading there but also a warning. He wanted to reach out, to speak, but something in him ... refused. He was stubborn, he would not bend no matter the plea.

*Heed me.*

Petulantly, the Outcast turned away. He was almost awake now, for the first time in many years. Or perhaps not. He only stirred when time sat still, when the world whined on its track. He stirred only with the war wind. He was not beloved. He was unheard and unremembered. Forgotten, until the season of reaping and despair, until roots suckled on seas of blood.

The voice rose on the wind. There were no words to it now, merely force of will. It pushed, jostling, shaking him from the dark. The Outcast growled in anger, trying to resist. He was still strong and his roots stretched deep. But the voice was his voice now. It was in the air and the water and the soil. It was the moisture that nourished and the wind that ripped loose. Old Man Splinter gripped at the darkness nonetheless, even as the shadows slipped away, caught in the whirlwind of sensation.

*Up cruel one. Up, wilding. Up, outcast.*
*Awaken.*
*Awaken Old Man Splinter.*

The Outcast shuddered and with a moan to shake the ages, bark cracked and sap boiled like blood through open wounds. The tortured sound filled the empty space. He was awake.

The howl set the crows in the upper branches to flight, and caused Zhegra to snarl in agitation. It had come from close by. Too close for comfort. She twisted in her saddle, searching for the source. But, rather than having one point of origin, it seemed to echo from everywhere and nowhere all at once. It slithered between the trees to fill the empty silence of the writhing weeds and shifting insects. It was like a rumble of thunder, or the growl of an avalanche. 'Steady," she called, as her warriors stumbled back, muttering. "Form up."

Even with the comforting, sickly light that spilled from their torches, the darkness felt as if it were pressing on them. "These bloody trees swallow the light." Bhegrin rumbled. "We should cast them back and reveal the horrors with perfect clarity." The words sounded good but the dark remained and the echoes of the wail as well. What had it been? Some animal, surely no Drau had ever made that noise! There were beasts a plenty in a place like this. But no beast screamed like that.

Despite her bravado, she could see her warriors crowd together. Their voices were but a dim rumble. The hound-master assured them that they had not made a wrong turn. He at least was convinced of the fact that he had not lead them astray. She looked around. There were bones of men and monsters filling the hollows within the roots - a stark reminder that theirs were not the first feet to attempt to push through. Every Dwentari felt the choking weight of sap-laced air seeking to smother them. Bhegrin used his broken-tipped sword to chop a path through the tangled density of the forest. Others did the same, hacking the branches and roots which seemed to almost rise up in opposition.

Zhegra longed to topple the trees, and burn their roots to ash. But that was a fool's game. They could burn every tree here and make no impact on these knotted eves. *Was it that the woods grew larger because she was in it*, she wondered.

Branches cracked and splintered in the dark, noises separate from the thud of axes and the rattle of swords. Unseen things were moving past them, flowing away ahead, to where? Zhegra peered into the dark. What were they fleeing from - her, or something else? Again, she wondered at what the oracle had not told her, what she had 'seen'. She shook her head, banishing her fears. "We are the hunters, not the hunted," she murmured and Razortooth quivered encouragingly.

"Almost there, my lady." The hound-master managed encouragingly, trudging alongside. "We caught another one around here." His head twisted as something scurried through the undergrowth. "Always on the run," he added shaking his head.

Zhegra grunted and manoeuvred the Sithaxi around a cloven tree. The air was vibrating now with a bone-deep throb that set her teeth on edge. It was as if the noise had been but a prelude. The lizard-beast snapped softly. She looked up, eyes narrowed.

Something shone, out in the dark. At first, she thought it was more torches, but it lacked the oily sheen and fatty stench. Instead, it put her in mind of sunlight reflected off mountain slopes. Zhegra's lip curled. The trees were filled with sound now, even the steady march of her warriors was obscured. The trees shuddered as if caught in a hurricane wind, and the shadows danced. With a shake of her head, she kicked the sithaxi into a run, Bhegrin and the hound-master in her wake, his hounds yelping and scuttling about him.

Zhegra slowed as she reached the edges of the light, and lifted Razortooth in a signal to halt as she dismounted. Sliding from the saddle she lifted the chain-link reigns over the sithaxi's head, ignoring its attempts to bite. It was nervous. She understood. The light soft as it was, stung the eyes and skin even though she raised her axe arm to shield herself. The canopy over-head was so thick that true light couldn't pierce its shadowed recesses.

The trees at the edges of the clearing bent outwards, as if pushed away from an edifice which occupied its grassy heart. Even the roots were humped and coiled, like great anacondas. Zhegra approached with caution. There were stones here and there, she did not speak Rhegarsi, the native tongue of the Drau, but she knew a warding stone when she saw one. Such monoliths should have stood tall and proud, witchery designed to keep whatever dwelt here, contained. These were toppled - deliberately.

The stones were large, many hands taller than her gaunt sithaxi she could not see where the others were. A trickle of water poured down from some unseen source and turned the mossy ground soft and spongy. This vibrant green moss now covered the calves of the trees that dwelt here and had begun to crawl across the stones also. Carefully, she reached down and began to pull clumps of it away. A small part of her screamed a warning, though the markings were unlike any dread symbol or bane marking she was familiar with. What ever they were, Razortooth was eager to deface them.

The axe seemed to strain in her hands like one of the hounds, the barbs in its haft digging painfully into her palm. Some instinct held her back. If they stormed this glade, whatever was watching them would scatter and vanish. The forest would swallow them up, and even the hound-master wouldn't be able to track them. So, the choice was made up for her. Leave them. Let them start whatever they had come to this place to do. Then, and only then, would come the time to strike.

They rested, lying low in the undergrowth and waited. As one the trio of Drau sentries appeared from between the trees. Not the type she had seen in battle, nor the dark shadowy ones that had stalked them since their retreat. These were toughened, some even scarred, and each bearing unique war gear presumably pertaining to their preference, and lightly if at all armoured - at least by Dwentari comparison. Zhegra watched as the trio kept close while one dragged the dismembered head of a boar across the branch and roots of the next tree, leaving thick strings of coagulating blood behind. They muttered to each other as they worked, softly at first growing louder and more urgent.

"What are they doing?" Bhegrin mumbled, pointing to the wet splashes of blood and viscera. Zhegra slipped back to her sithaxi and slid back into the saddle. Leaves rose, cast into the air by the wind. She shook her head. "Who can say," she replied. "Their shaman rituals are none of our concern. Take them now."

Zhegra kicked the sithaxi in the sides and charged out from the thickened trees towards the trio of preoccupied Drau. "For the Iron Lord!" she wailed, Razortooth singing with a voice only she could hear. Eagerly, she swung down on the nearest Drau, splitting it's skull in a welter of bone and brain matter. The woman toppled with a rattling cry cut short as the blade was torn loose.

She jerked on the sithaxi's reigns, turning the steed about. "They are trying to confuse us and keep us in this wretched place. Teach them their folly," she shouted turning the sithaxi around and charging as two more Drau lurched out of the forest, seeking to defend their friends. The one in the lead was far quicker than the others, more spry and lean with weather worn skin and a bespoke blade of silvered steel. Zhegra though that this was surely a lord of some kind though its mismatched attire looked too barbarian in comparison to others she had met. He strode to meet her, its followers swarming like angry hornets in its wake, every step measured and precisely taken.

As he came close, picking up speed, he reached out and tossed heavy corded bolas. They spun towards her like striking serpents and tangled about the sithaxis legs. The lizard-beast issued an undulating call and lashed out before toppling onto its side, biting and whatever came close - friend or foe. Zhegra leaped from the saddle, landing heavily upon a split log. She turned and struck down with Razortooth, hacking at the binds that entwined the beasts legs. The axe vibrated in her grip, pleased to be of use. A moment later the wilding hero was upon her.

The silvered blade scythed through the air, scraping across the front of her armour. The force of the blow nearly knocking her back. Zhegra laughed, despite the bruised pain. "Yes, yes! Fight me witch-spawn," she roared, spinning Razortooth about. She sliced a divet out of her opponents exposed shoulder, the flesh tearing open against the bite of the serrated blade. It staggered back, clutching it's arm with an agonized wheeze that sounded like branches clattering in a wind-storm. Blood poured from between his fingers. Speaking something utterly alien it swung out its sword like a talon, and Zhegra was forced to turn aside as her victim sent a storm of lesser blows in her direction.

Out of the corner of her eye she could see Bhegrin, his flail whirling above his head. The Drau target of his intent, turned aside more swiftly than Zhegra would have thought possible, avoiding the blow. A pair of whips snapped out from the Drau's waist and Bhegrin was snatched from his feet. He cried out her name, but to no avail. The second whip tightened about his neck, and wrung the Dwentari like a wet rag, crushing his throat till his mouth foamed blood. The Drau flung the body aside and turned as Zhegra gave a hate-filled cry and charged.

The whips struck out again, arrowing towards her. They struck against her armour, seeking the seams and joins that kept her encased. Behind her the sithaxi screamed and hissed in pain as two Drau leaped upon its flank, stabbing down with sharp, paired knives. It bucked and roared, trying to shake it's attackers loose. The moment's diversion was all her opponent needed as one whip snapped about her arm. She reached up with Razortooth, trying to cut her way free but the plaited leather was tough as old sinew.

"Leave her, wild thing," The loyal hound-master barrelled into the side of the whip-wielding Drau with wild abandon, a rusted blade carving easily through the petty pieces of leather armour. The Drau issued a scream as the hounds burbled and worried at their legs and arms. It yelled some heathen war-cry and slammed its forehead into the face of the hound-master, swatting the stunned Dwentari from it and punching one of his dogs squarely in the snout. The Drau picked itself up.

"A mistake," Zhegra said, with a guttural laugh. "I am the one you should be worried about, little brute."

The sithaxi leaped to her protectively, its maw hung with flesh and pieces of muscle. She swung into what remained of its saddle and the lizard-beast surged forwards, driving its way toward the Drau with a speed that belied its girth. Zhegra swung Razortooth in a decapitating strike, narrowly missing its face. It pulled away with a feral yell before the blow could fall. Luck, more than anything saved its life.

The Drau stumbled away from him, clutching its ruined hand and half falling back over a gnarled root. It sank down moaning hoarsely, it's mauled arm coated in blood. It would never swing another whip again, that as much was certain. Glancing around, the other Drau were melting back between the trees, retreating as quickly as they could with the hounds in pursuit. Satisfied that it was all but finished,

Zhegra turned. She saw the hound-master hack the head from one still struggling Drau as it tried to crawl away. Blood burst across the leaves and soil. A few of her kin had fallen, but not so many that they did not still pose a threatening force, at least not at close quarters, and they had not died alone. Dripping Drau bodies lay broken and twisted across the glade.

She felt some relief in finding that the sithaxi was still capable of travel. The lizard-beast had taken heavy damage to its left hind leg but the blood was already clotting and the heavy gashes were even now beginning to scab. Sithaxi were hardy creatures, bred specifically, in large ranches all across the ash plains on the other side of the mountain. This one seemed particularly determined.

The vibratory song of the forest drifted, panting like a wounded animal. Zhegra looked back and cursed as she realised that a trail of blood led out of the glade from the mutilated Drau. Evidently, it had not been as wounded as she had thought. "Hunt the wounded one down," Zhegra snarled, angry at herself. "I want the bastards head for my trophy rack. It must pay for taking Bhegrin's life." *And for denying me the joy of killing it*, she thought savagely.

"We'll strip the flesh from what ever passes for its soul, my lady," the hound-master said, whistling to his hounds. They yelped and bounded between the trees with the stench of its blood in their nose, excited to finish the job they'd started. Zhegra knew how they felt.

She looked down and gestured to one of her kin. "You," she called pointing to a sister warrior with scalp of intricate tattoos."

"Chuulat," she replied, inclining her head.

Zhegra nodded. "Chuulat, see what other of these damnable stones you can find. The Draurhegar have seen fit to ward this place and I am for the hunt." She thudded her heels into the sithaxi's flanks and urged her steed after the hound-master. A number of others followed her, ignoring Chuulat's raspy commands to stay. Zhegra laughed. She was inclined to leniency. After all, their blood was up and they too required vengeance.

"Come my brothers and sisters," she shouted, still laughing. "Let us see what prey awaits us!"

In his delirium, Old Man Splinter called out. He cast his voice into the teeth of the world, listening as it echoed through the shadows and knotholes. The wind carried his call and living things shrank back. It echoed in the secret places where sane things feared to tread. He was not alone her realised. There were other things here, he could feel the vibration of them through the ground. Broken things, with cracked souls and minds riven with hunger and malice.

Inside the gnarled pulp of his flesh, he felt a biting hunger. Something had been suppressed but the bonds that had held him to rest were some how loosened. Buzzing voices murmured to him as children to a father. They sought comfort and reassurance, but that was not something he could give. The barbs of his roots were parched and the sap veins within him had turned dusty and dry. In anger he growled. He was awake now and his awareness had returned. He had been starved and his limbs were weak but... there was something, a tasty morsel to revive his ancient form.

With the cracking of ancient wood and tearing soil he strode the root road through the shadows, at once insubstantial and implacable. Blood. He could smell it. The sweet nectarine stench of the viciously rent and deliciously rich. His roots shook with a need to bathe in it and an anger that he had not been the one to see it severed. Memories muttered deep inside him, the intent lost beneath the swell of murmurings. He twitched, trying to see through the murk of memories and find the trail of the now.

Something had happened. That was all the Outcast had known. The Drau. Yes. The Drau had caste him hear and set him to sleep, though it had taken many of them to do so. So, yes, something had changed. They had released him, but for what purpose? He shrieked again, in frustration now, rather than command. He could feel the edges of that black moment in the air and the soil, like a wound that would not heal. It reverberated through him, searing his mind and filling him with dread purpose. The Drau would pay for his incarceration, but first he would feed. He was not dead yet. Not yet, and never again. He, Old Man Splinter would not allow it.

The thought snagged, uncomfortably close to epiphany. The Outcast remembered a time when he would drink deep of the lives in this forest. The needles of his roots and arms, piercing the veins of soft things to nourish the blood-wood. That was why he had been imprisoned, but no longer.

"It is time to hunt... to hunt... to hunt...," he hissed, the need swelling like a creek in a spring tide. Unnoticed until it is no longer ignorable, and then all-consuming, all at once. It raced through his branches, filling him with predatory instinct.

The trees quaked, they might have screamed if he'd stopped and listened. He saw them swaying in the wind, their roots stretching deeper and deeper. Their leaves twitched back, afraid to touch him. He was anathema. *Silly, dense things*, he didn't want their cold toughened dirt. He yearned for softer, warmer flesh. The forest feared him, and rivers receded at his approach. Animals and insects fell silent in his wake, root-claws gouging at the earth as he stalked forwards. New growths were beginning to push past his tattered form, growing and unfolding. Scything talons of bark and stone and vine sprout, swell, and flatten. They would tear and crush bone. By now he was singing, pulling himself through shuddering trees, leaving tiny scratches on their trembling bark to remind them - the blood-wood, Old Man Splinter had returned and he was hungry.

"Remember me... Remember this moment," he cooed, as the forest began to scream. He wallowed in their wailing and stopped. An agonised bellow crept through the air. The song on his cracked lips faltered, interrupted. He stood, still as death and listened as its last noted hung suspended, quavering, on the wind.

"You have called, and I am coming," he croaked, loping onwards eagerly. "I am here... I hunt... I slay... Remember."

Old Man Splinter laughed and the forest fell silent, abashed. Then, a sigh of noise filled the emptiness, like a soft, black whisper. Others like him. They had heard his song and found it to their liking. They were small, barely seedlings, but they had waited an age for his command and now they trailed towards him with reckless abandon.

The Outcast did not slow till he reached the glade, where the bars of his prison had once stood. The old stones are toppled and other things were creeping at the edges of his domain. Old Man Splinter did not know these creatures, they were new, strange, and the stain they left upon the dirt was like rotten fruit. Still, beggars could not be choosers. This was where the blood was. He could see it now, coating the leaves and dripping against the moss. Some of the meat sacks had already been tapped and his own branches shook with anger that these new creatures had spoilt so much of the feast.

He watched these defilers, the rotten ones, the grub-men, through his many eyes, hidden by the thorns and briars. They were small, compared to him, and their souls were weak things, flickering on the edge of awareness. Every bird and branch was caught in silent terror of his appearance, but these creatures, these could not hear it. They were deaf to danger, though they lacked any knowledge of their handicap. But he would show them.

The Outcast burst upon them is a shower of shattered bark and drifting leaves as if tearing through the veil of the world. The meat-sacks were slow to react, slow to understand the monster in their midst. The muscle of his roots and limbs lash out. Unable to contain himself or his strength, he tore the head from the first misting the air in blood. A groan of ecstasy passed from him as the bright liquid spattered his joints, greasing them with renewed life. One by one his capillaries opened and drank it from the air, dozens of starving mouths licking the life-blood from him as he reached for the next.

Dull pain crawled across his gnarled bark from the bite of metallic teeth. Wood split, sap oozed and a deafening scream. His arms swung, snatching the dirty grub-man from the ground and raising it still struggling to the serrated gash of his widening mouth as easily as he might snatch a worm from the soil. The fleshy thing's scream was snapped short as he splintered teeth sang into its neck. Rich and thick, the life-blood poured down the Outcast's throat, caught in rapture, he gulped and sucked hungrily but too soon the thing was a dry husk and he tossed its saggy exterior to one side. It collided into another of its kind, smashing both against the nearest tree with a crack of bone and gristle. They were so fragile these piles of meat and muscle. So ephemeral. A bundle of scattered moments soon forgotten.

With two of their number destroyed the flesh-things charged at Old Man Splinter. He felt the hack and saw of their retribution but he was old, ancient even and his iron-bark would not yield so easily. "I am the blood-wood... I will not hide. I will hunt... I will slay... I will drink. The trees here will grow fat again on red water," he hissed, skewering two more on the end of a talon.

He drew up to his full height through a storm of leaves and branches. This forest had been his prison, a place to hide his monstrousness, ashamed. Animals squealed and stamped as he ravaged through the meat-sack men, snapping their brittle bones and tearing away the skin to get at the pulsing hearts beneath. Their blood was piquant now, spiced and heady with the taste of fear and terror. So much mulch to quench his thirst.

Old Man Splinter could not stand the shrill screams of the meat. There was no song to it. Their squeak and scream was too fast and too high. *Why do they talk so much, he wondered. Why do they clog the air with words and sound the of meat slapping against meat?* He desired only a grave silence and a bountiful river of red. *Fragile... so fragile*, he thought, as he pulled away another head, uncorking the fizzing supply beneath. In thought he pulled the meat-man apart, stripping the flesh and muscle and bone, one red blossom at a time. The meat-man fell silent, his writhing subdued to a haphazard twitch. Bit of its flesh dangled from his claws, but the Outcast lost interest in it quickly.

They flee, rather run than face him. With a spasm of muscle, Old Man Splinter felt his roots reach out, churning through the bloody soil. The slowest was snagged by their needle-teeth and dragged down. Each vicious tooth pierced the flesh and the root bulged and pulsed as it fed while the meat-man screamed and its friends fled. The Outcast ignored them, dragging his prey back across the forest floor to continue his butchery. They would lose themselves in this forest. The saplings would drag them down into the dark. That was their pleasure. Like him, they had been hidden beneath the canopy, trapped and starving, until the reaping came again.

The last of the meat-men dangled from his claws, ruined. He had drained it to a husk. Satiated for this moment at least, Old Man Splinter turned and stopped. For a moment he could hear the song of the forest, soothing and soft. It was... familiar. A broken body moaned against the floor and the spell was broken. A root snatched the meat into the ground and he could feel the thing shaking as the teeth turn it to powder. For a moment he had almost forgotten... no. He would never forget and never remember. There was only the thirst and the smell of blood on the wind.

Old Man Splinter threw back his head and shrieked.

The Drau was gone.

A bloody trail had marked its stumbling flight. It had sought the trees to hide, but the hounds had found it and followed it regardless. They had lead Zhegra and the others on a yelping chase, away from the glade and the hateful light of the stones. Bloody hand prints and smears lead them deeper into the dark and the quiet of the forest, until the only light was their torches and the only sound was the crunch of dead leaves.

But their quarry was nowhere to be found. Even the hound-master seemed to have lost the trail, and his dogs now circled and yelped in apparent confusion. Zhegra cursed and smacked a fist on the saddle. Some part of her had expected as much. "Where is the bloody bastard? It can't have gotten far. Not with the wounds I gave it," she said.

Before the hound-master could reply, a monstrous shriek echoed through the forest. The yelping hounds fell silent and clunk back towards their master, tails tucked between their legs. The shriek seemed to grow in strength, reverberating in the dark, before finally fading away. Zhegra gripped Razortooth more tightly. "What was that?" She looked this way and that, turning the sithaxi around and around. "Why does it not come out if it wishes to challenge us?" She stood in the saddle and peered into the dark. For a moment she thought she saw something move beneath a shroud of roots, but dismissed the idea. *A serpent,* she thought. *Or some weak creature, seeking to hide from them.*

"The hounds don't like it, my lady." The hound-master peered into the trees warily. "This is something new. The smell... it is not a Drau."

Zhegra nodded. She was no tracker but even she could feel the tone of the forest shift. Her thoughts drifted back to the toppled stones. Perhaps whatever sorcery lingered in them had drifted into the soil, but it did not seem likely. And it was everywhere, and growing stronger. Like hint of rain, heralding a storm.

The smell wasn't the whole of it. The trees were trembling but not from fear, though there had been fear for sure, this was the jitter of anticipation. As if the forest was a wounded animal and it was about to turn on its hunters. They were crowding them. She made a hand signal, urging those with her to back away. A predator was coming, though she could not say why she thought that until she thought about the blood. "They were baiting it," she growled, angry at not having realised it sooner. "What ever creature the bastards kept here, they were leading it to us."

For the first time in a long time, Zhegra felt what might have been the embers of an old and forgotten sensation - fear. The sithaxi was silent and the hounds had begun to whimper, the sounds from her warriors were little better. She rolled her shoulders, trying to shake away the uncomfortable feeling. They had faced the sorcerous legions of the Draurhegar, scaled the icy teeth of their frozen goddess, but here, now, she could feel her courage stretch thin. The joy they had felt at the hunt a moment ago, had turned to silence.

"We should go back," the hound-master whispered. "Whatever

ritual bound those stones is shattered. Evil stirs. We should regroup with the others."

Zhegra ground her teeth in frustration. In the dark, something laughed. The hounds began to bay shrilly and her sithaxi hissed and scratched. "Light - more light," Zhegra snapped. She reached down and snatched a crackling torch from an outstretched hand. The warrior yelled and held fast as if his life depended upon it. Until, in a tug of war, it rolled across the carpet of roots. The ground was too wet for it to catch.

More laughter. Something peered at her from behind a tree. Zhegra twisted in her saddle, but whatever it was, it was gone. Chuckles echoed down like raindrops. Childish laughter slithered up from the roots. Zhegra could hear wood scrape against wood. She caught a glimpse of shifting bark but never in the same place twice.

"Steady my kin," Zhegra murmured, as she tried to control her restive steed. "We are the hunters, not some big cat or summoned beast." As she spoke, the laughter ceased. Silence fell.

Then, crackling. Not of fire, but like twigs snapping. One of her warriors gestured with his blade. "I saw something," he started. "By that tree." Zhegra looked. The tree was gnarled and stunted, sheared almost in half. In the flickering glare of the fallen torch she could make out something moving, many things. They shifted like ghosts through the gloom.

With a cackling shriek, the warrior was snatched sideways by unseen arms Flesh popped and tore as the warrior's torn head trundled across the ground. Anarchy broke out. A moment later and another was yanked upwards, into the shadowy canopy, legs kicking until a shower of red gore and the sound of gargling proclaimed his death.

Dwentari were a blessed people, granted strength and durability, forged in iron and stone as the mountains had made them, but none of those gifts mattered here. The cyclone of stabbing claws and gnashing fangs tore even the most doughty brother or sister to bloody ruin. "Back, fall back," Zhegra roared. She lashed out to gouge at her unseen attacker but met nothing but air. A barbed, talon-like branch struck out at her sithaxi. "Leave me," Zhegra yelled, taking it off at the knuckle with a clean sweep." A shadow fell over her and she looked up into the face of an aged man, its face taught across bones of root and vine. It struck at her, teeth like splinters tearing into the neck of the sithaxi. The lizard-thing shrilled in agony, twisting and snapping with its own fangs. Zhegra swept her axe out, hacking at the creature savagely. It issued a screeching, scratching sound and retreated before Razortooth's bite, but only for a moment.

Zhegra hauled on the sithaxi's reigns, turning her steed about. It lumbered painfully, wheezing and slow from blood loss. "Fall back to the stones," she bellowed. She couldn't say whether any of them heard her. She bisected a snaking, toothed root and turned the sithaxi away, racing through the forest and bent low over it's neck.

There were few things that the Dwentari and the Draurhegar shared. The two peoples hated each other unreservedly, but Zhegra had heard tales of blood crazed monsters who lurked in the dark places of the world. Twisted misinterpretations of nature, more savage and cruel than a rabid sithaxi. Old things. If such creatures infested these lands it was no wonder that the Iron Lord desired their taming.

If she could make it back to the stones she might yet be able to mount a defence. Zhegra looked around, trying to spot the light of the stones, but she saw only darkness, or the brief, bounding motion of a torch swiftly snuffed. She wondered whether the hound-master was one of those. She'd lost lost sight of the old Dwentari in the attack. If they were to leave this cursed place, she hoped that he was still alive.

As soon as the thought crossed her mind, she heard a cry of pain or perhaps a challenge. Zhegra turned the sithaxi about, pursuing the sound, the lizard-beast snapped in protest. "Hound-Master! Hold fast - I am coming," she shouted. If anyone could find their way back to the stones it would be him.

"This way my lady," The hound-master's voice called out and Zhegra saw a spark of light.

"Hurry! This way..." She pointed the sithaxi towards the flickering light of the hound-masters torch. When she reached its light, she saw the torch on the ground, and the hound-master standing just out of sight, gesturing to her. *What was the fool doing? Trying to hide behind a tree?* Zhegra grimaced. Perhaps he was injured.

"Hound-master? What-?" Zhegra began. The hound-master made a horrid, wet sound and what was left of him staggered into the light. His flesh had been perforated at a hundred points by thin needles of bark, which stretched back towards the creature following close behind him. It grinned wickedly at them and manipulated the root making the hound-master stumble like a marionette. One bone white length caught his sagging features, squeezing his mouth open. As it did so, it said, "This... way... this... way," in a raspy approximation of the Dwentari tongue.

Zhegra watched in revulsion as the creature made the hound-master dance a merry jig, scattering droplets of blood around and around. The Dwentari groaned pitiably as the toothed roots jerked his body this way and that. Then, with a final mocking cackle, the creature hunched forwards, its roots wrapping and contorting around its prey and tore the hound-master apart in a welter of steaming gore. The sight of his demise snapped Zhegra from her fugue and she drove her heels into the sithaxi's sides. The sithaxi screamed and fled.

Enraged Zhegra urged the lizard-beast to greater speed. Branches and leaves turned to powder beneath its thundering paws. But no matter how fast her steed ran, she could still hear the creature just behind her. Suddenly, the sithaxi fell hissing and shrieking and Zhegra was hurled from the saddle. She scrambled to her feet, a broken rib scraping her heaving lungs. The sithaxi kicked and snapped in distress as roots burrowed into the muscles of its legs. spines of dark, bloody wood speared from the lizard-beasts abused flesh, shredding its tattered hide.

The sithaxi snapped blindly at the air as its scales began to slick with its own blood. More roots snaked around it, restraining its thrashing form, as it sought to rise. Until, the sithaxi's movements lessened and runnels of blood began to absorb as if lapped by a grotesquely long tongue.

"No, no, no," Zhegra wheezed as she stumbled towards Razortooth, embedded in a stump during her fall. She jerked the axe free and jerked back towards her faithful steed. Vainly, she chopped at the vines and roots. But it was useless. Almost all of the sithaxi was shrouded in pulsing roots, devoured from the inside out. "Up, get up," Zhegra cried, trying to tear the roots away from the steeds neck and jaw. "Fight it, you stupid beast... fight..." she trailed off. Only one of the lizard-beasts eyes was visible now, glazed and staring. She could still just about hear the sithaxi's laboured and agonised hiss. Zhegra laid her hand on the side of the steeds head. "I am sorry," she whispered.

Then, crying out with rage, she brought Razortooth down on the sithaxi's skull. The lizard- beast gave one thrash, then stilled. Zhegra tore her axe free and turned away. She limped through the trees, not caring whether she was going the right way or not. Sometimes she heard screams and occasionally, the pained shrieks of one of the poor hounds. But mostly, she heard the laughter whenever she dared to slow.

Blood and phlegm leaked from her when she at last staggered back into the glade. She shouted for her kin, but received no reply. Blearily, she scanned the surround. The area was the sight of a catastrophe. Branches and trees had snapped and the ground was broken. Something impossibly large had stormed through here. There was no sign of the warriors she had left behind save for a sword embedded in the ground. As she drew close she recognised it as Bhegrin's blade. Roots clung to it and as she watched in sickened fascination, they drew the sword down into the dark soil until it was completely lost to sight.

Zhegra looked down. She caught glimpses of serrated armour plate and twitching fingers beneath the leaves, and suspicious hummocks of moss that might have been bodies. The sound of branches creaked above her but she didn't look around. It was taunting her.

"I do not fear you. This is the moment I was created for," Zhegra said, lifting Razortooth. But her words sounded hollow, and her axe shuddered fearfully in her grip. *I am not afraid. I am Shield-Lady of Kherdrom and I am not afraid,* she thought. The ground undulated beneath her feet. "I am not afraid - my moment has come! Come, come and die, monster," she shouted, turning slowly. "Where are you?"

Screams were her only reply. The screams of her kin, as something hurt them, deep in the dark. The whine of crumpling armour, the crunching of bone as something fed. Whatever was out there was laughing as it spilt seas of sour blood. But there was no humour in the sound, no joy. She turned. A branch snapped behind her.

Zhegra spun. A blow smashed her from her feet. Somehow she managed to hold on to Razortooth, and use the haft of the axe to lever herself upright. The thing followed her as she rose and stumbled back. How had she not seen it before? How could such a creature hide? Had it been stalking them this entire time? It was like nothing she had seen before, a hideous, monstrous tree. It towered over her. Long, bestial limbs sprouted horrid waxy red leaves across a surface that was swelling and contracting constantly. Long, flat talons dripping with gore, flexed as if in anticipation. But its face was the worst of all, at once humanoid and monstrous in its nest of thorny locks.

That hideous head cocked, watching him. Motes of red, like hot embers hovered for eyes and the blood of her brothers and sisters ran down from its splinter-like fangs. She swallowed the scream that tried to break from her lips. Razortooth whimpered in her hands, and she knew the axe was afraid.

The moment stretched taught. The abomination lifted a claw. Zhegra recognised what was left of the hunt-master's face, twisting on a talon tip.

"For the Iron Lord," she whispered, her voice growing in strength. "For the Silver Fortress!" She lunged, Razortooth raised. A blow rocked her back on her heels. A second lifted her into the air.

Razortooth slipped from her numb fingers as she hurtled backwards. Her back struck something unyielding, and she felt something crack. The warmth of the stone spread through her, and she clawed uselessly at the ground, trying to move away from the creature. The soil twitched and broke, long knifed roots snaring her, dragging her down to the mincing fangs beneath. Soil filled her mouth and she gagged. Her legs didn't work. The roots tightened pressing against her, seeking a way beneath her armour. It murmured to her in a grinding voice she could not understand.

Desperate now, remembering what had happened to her sithaxi, Zhegra tore an arm free and groped for Razortooth's haft. If she could reach her axe... if... if... if. Wood creaked and the stench of old blood filled her nose. The abomination watched her, sitting back on its haunches. It reached out a claw and touched Razortooth.

The axe made a sound like a wounded cat as more thin roots rose up it's haft and slid into the wood. The haft cracked and bust. The blade, blessed by the Oracle herself, lay avoided and ignored. Zhegra wondered if anyone would find it or would it be there forever, a small mark in this verdant hell?

Zhegra looked back up into the dull eyes of her killer, and saw a most beautiful despair there. Like her it had surrendered. Not to sorcery as she had first thought but perhaps to something worse, for its surrender had brought it no comfort. There was no joy in it's eyes. Zhegra felt her body grow cold. And when the first roots pierced her armour and the flesh beneath, she smiled in contentment.

Old Man Splinter watched the last of the meat-men vanish beneath the soil to its waiting roots and yet he felt no satisfaction, only hunger. He wondered what the strange creatures of his domain had been saying in their strange hummingbird voice, too high and swift to understand. A curse perhaps? He knew all about curses, for he had been wreathed in them. They inundated him and strengthened him, he was a curse.

Out of the corner of his eye something moved. He twitched his leaves preparing to strike. The Drau was not afraid, she was armoured but bore no weapon and unlike others, he can hear her voice. *The reaping is passed, it is time to fade.*

The Outcast looked up and tried to block her words from its mind.

*The reaping has passed, Old Man Splinter. Cease and sleep.*

Old Man Splinter stiffened. The fires of his fury, growing anew. He remembers now. He will not sleep. He will not be imprisoned. He will feed. No, he will not go back to sleep. He looked at her, still mumbling her incantations, thinking that she had this power over him. Small, silly, young creature. He had been ancient before her grandmothers' were born.

A roar, like a forest fire crashed through the forest, its weight like an avalanche as something incredibly old and incredibly dark called.

And it was angry...

# Superstition

"Sleep, or repose that deserved the name of sleep, was out of the question."
—Jane Austen, Northanger Abbey

"Dead?"

The word was more of a question than a statement, expressed more with curiosity than with emotion. Arryn Vheadra hated the way her sister, Shael, spoke - cold and acidic, making her words less an observation more than audible sneer. She had a manner of making even the darkest moments in life just that little bit more unpleasant by injecting a tone of bitterness and contempt.

The body dumped within the alley didn't care. It was past such mundane things. Death had rendered it immune to Shael's morbid humour. Arryn turned the corpse over to see the vicious slashes across its torso. *You'd have thought that with the war, the Drau would have more pressing things to occupy their time*, she thought, checking over the wounds. The chest looked more like something out of a butchers shop, two of the wounds carved so deep that they'd hit bone. Shael was leaning over her like some macabre bird of prey. "I imagine that would be enough to kill someone," she quipped, wrinkling her nose at the gruesome sight. "What do you think? Robbery gone wrong?"

Arryn shook her head. "He still has his coin purse." She held up the clinking leather pouch. A gasp echoed from behind them and Shael's posture stiffened. At the end of the alley a small crowd was beginning to form. It brought a wry grin to Arryn's face. Death wasn't uncommon in the city, least not these days. Everyone liked a good old fashioned murder. It was practically a spectator sport. Still, it was fun to watch Shael's discomfort play across her sharp, almost cadaverous features.

"I'd say that the wounds were made by a sword or fine blade," Arryn continued.

"Nonsense!" Shael protested. "He's been cut up like a joint for roasting."

Arryn made an expansive gesture with her arm, indicating the street beyond. The rest of the alley that lead to it was littered with a motley collection of oddments - coils of rope, scraps of cheap cloth, bits and pieces of battered tinware. The shattered remains of a cart leaned at the entrance to the street, it's yoke had cracked presumably when it had struck the corner of the building, but other than that was still serviceable. "Why would anyone leave this loot just lying around?" She stood and walked towards the wagon. Shael followed just behind her.

The similarity between them was striking. Were it not that Shael stood half a head taller than her sister, one might have confused them for twins - once upon a time. Now, a thin scar that was still a livid red crossed from hairline to cheek on Arryn's face, blinding her in one eye. A parting gift from a Dwentari soldier from her time on the front line in a war that was still ongoing. She had returned. She could not say the same for too many of her friends. She had been lucky.

"I think I know a thing or two about sword wounds to know one when I see it." She pointed a finger back to the body. "You should know a few things too. Go and take a look for yourself if you don't trust me."

Shael scowled, her sharp features displaying the disgust her sister's suggestion provoked. Warily, she cast a glance at the corpse, then turned away. "I'll take your word for it," she grumbled and pushed past Arryn, retrieving a clay bottle from beneath the wooden drivers seat of the cart. With practised ease, she removed the stopper with a thumb and pressed the vessel to her lips. "I've no stomach for that kind of work any more. The Dhal-Marrah's saw to that."

"So you hide in a bottle now?" Arryn challenged.

Shael arched an eyebrow. "And you? Is your hiding place any purer than mine. We've both seen our share of blood. Don't demoralize me sister, I know you too well for that."

The pair glared at each other, the last shreds of dignity and self-respect struggling to assert themselves. It was a battle that was lost before it had even started. Neither of them had enough honour left to argue, not least because both of them were in some shape or form, right. Arryn was hiding from the ghosts of the past, from things she had done, things she should have done. Hindsight was the most terrible curse the goddess could lay upon a Drau's mind.

"When you're done deciding if you want to wring my neck," Shael said, "you might want to take a look at what our dead friend has left behind." She lowered her tone. "Perhaps some of it is worth selling."

"Don't we have enough already?" Arryn asked, waving her hand to covered wagon on the other side of the street. The bed of it was already loaded with dented helms and rusty bits of armour, notched swords, and discarded bric-a-crab. The pile represented the pickings of the city's less desirable locations. Shael was a scavenger as cunning as any vulture, seemingly able to smell out a fresh corpse a league away.

Or perhaps that was giving her too much credit. With east-side rife with plague and the steady bleed of returning soldiers from the warfront passing through the southern gates, it didn't take exceptional skill to find death. The Goddess Eroth had reaped a grim harvest of her children from the shores of Darktide to the western marshes, depopulating entire villages and turning towns into diseased charnel houses. Arryn felt her gorge rise at the obscenities which were part and parcel of the war between the Draurhegar and the Dwentari of the south. Ostensibly, the two sisters were wandering peddlers, selling second-hand goods. Exactly how they procured their wares was something their patrons were were better off not knowing.

"The high houses have the fattest purses in the land," Shael said. "Are you suggesting that we poor vagabonds are more altruistic then them?"

"Save the speech," Arryn replied, her voice bitter with shame. She started gathering up the rubbish littering the road as the crowd dispersed, wanting nothing to do with them now it was clear what they were about.

"Don't forget his pockets," Shael called.

"Do your own dirty work," Arryn snapped, folding up a ratty sheet of linen.

Shael stared back at the corpse, her face twisted with revulsion. She took a swallow from the bottle. Wiping beads of alcohol from her lower lip, she turned her gaze to her sister. "We're going to have to discuss our working arrangement. I think you've forgotten who's in charge."

"You need me more than I need you," Arryn shot back. "How long do you think you'd last travelling from city to city?"

The suggestion caused Shael's skin to bleach of colour. She tried to brush aside the implied threat. "I can find other sell-swords."

Suddenly, the argument was forgotten as Arryn gestured excitedly to an object lying beneath the broken cart.

Shael responded with calculated slowness, knowing every moment of delay would infuriate Arryn. Eventually, she reached the cart, discarding the bottle at the mouth of the alley. Stooping, she crawled behind the cart wheel and dragged a heavy box out from under the wreck Her bony fingers stroked the tooled leather covering, eyes lingering over the gilt letters and the little silver clasp. The lettering meant nothing to her, but she could appreciate the finery of workmanship. She hadn't played the role of looter long enough to lose a thief's eye for valuables.

"Open it!" Arryn ordered.

Shael acted without reluctance, as eager as her sister to see what they had found. She fumbled with the clasp - locked.

"Give it here," Arryn held out her hand as Shael passed it up. She gave it a cursory glance and brought a dagger scratching behind the metal clasp. It was the work of a few moments to get the box open, the blade chewing into the expensive leather.

When the box was open, Shael snatched it back and uttered a snarl of outrage.

"Cut yourself?" Arryn wondered, barely able to withdrew the blade in time.

No," Shael hissed. Her lean hand dipped into the box and removed a bird-like mask. Arryn recognised the style as that employed by the wise folk, though she'd never seen one in black before.

"Any coin?" she asked.

"No," Shael repeated. "Nothing. Just a bunch of crude medical instruments and waxed gloves." She laughed bitterly, holding out the strange leather mask. "Our late friend appears to have fancied himself something of a physic. How ironic."

Arryn didn't understand the disgust in her sister's voice but then in the camps, they hadn't really had much in the way of medical professionals. A matron with a stock of bandages and a prayer on their was considered enough for the best of the Draurhegar.

"Quacks and charlatans," Shael spat. "Most of them wouldn't know a pimple from the pox. They fleece the desperate and the dying." She snapped the box shut. "It's profitable."

Arryn fixed her with a withering look. "Not getting ideas I hope."

Shael dropped it onto the bed of their wagon and pulled herself up into the driving seat. She barely waited long enough for Arryn to climb up beside her, before cracking the reins angrily and jolting down the street.

Cold rain hissed against roof tiles and the wagon sloshed in the muddy mire as it approached the main street of the next town. A trio of geese scattered before the hooves of the horse, cackling in protest as they darted through the gaps in wattle fences or disappeared between the spaces between half-buried, squat houses. A skinny dog wandered idly across their path, pausing to nose about in the mud until the wagon was almost upon it. It considered a patched cat, lazing in the brick doorway of a storehouse, and pawed it's way to the other side of the road as the two strangers rode deeper into town.

Of the inhabitants, there was no sign.

"This place looks abandoned," Shael murmured, her fingers drumming against the seat.

Arryn uttered a grim chuckle. "You should have seen the frontier villages by the mountains." Her voice dropped to a venomous pitch.

"Spend some time in the Dwentari warpath where death has been at work. You get to know what desolation looks like. The houses smashed in and ransacked, the streets strewn with garbage, wolves prowling about. There's a feeling to such places not easily forgotten and not easily mistaken."

"Then where are all the people?" Shael persisted. "We can't exactly sell to their pets." She looked across the buildings on either side of the road. Most of them were wattle or crude wooden shelters sinking into the mud with simple gabled roofs. Interspersed among the buildings was a confusion of allotments and animal shelters. Pig sties, bird coops, vegetable patches, a handful of goats were even in evidence, grazing on a nub of grassy ground bordered by a rough fence.

Arryn pressed a finger to her lips, motioning for her sister to be quiet. She turned her head to one side and closed her eyes. "Do you hear that?" she asked, a smug smile pulling across her face.

With her prompting, Shael found that she did hear a faint noise, a murmur of voices coming to them from some distance.

"They sound angry," Arryn offered.

"Good," Shael replied, pulling her soaked cloak further around her. "Angry people will be interested in what we have." She cast a despairing look across the sprawl of dwellings. "Whether any of them can afford it looks to be questionable."

The wagon rattled down the lane. Niether of them noticed the cat in the doorway suddenly spring to its feet, arching its back and spitting at something in the shadows beside the storehouse. The cat's fright sent it yowling off across the nearby cabbage patch.

Yellow eyes watched the animal flee, then returned their interest to the wagon. Only when it disappeared around the corner did the eyes withdraw, slipping back into darkness.

The wagon came to a stop when it reached the sprawling mire which seemed to serve as a town square. A big old oak tree, it's trunk stained by fungus and moss, loomed above the morass, a wooden gibbet swinging from one of its thickest branches. The crumbling remains of a skeleton still swayed, grinning down at the people below.

There was no question now as to where the townspeople had gone. The growling mob scattered about the square, numbered in their hundreds. Shael saw a ragged farmer brandish a pitchfork and a cluster of wizened women fashioning torches. There were a handful of soldiers in armour - little more than brigadine leathers sporting some obscure set of heraldry, but these worthies didn't seem inclined to stop the unrest. Far from it, their voices were among the loudest of the mob.

The focus of the violence was directed at a lone man dressed in black, trimmed with scarlet. A weighty chain hung from his neck. His outfit might have been fine but it was dappled with muck. Rocks, heads of cabbage, and even a live chicken were pelted at the man as he tried to read from a document clenched in his hands but a fresh barrage of rubbish forced him back.

"Take it back to the capital!" a snaggle-toothed half-breed declared.

"By order of the houses," the beleaguered messenger declared, "and the will of Eroth-"

"Tell it to my Regdil!" raged a shrivelled woman, her face contorted with pain and fury. "Tell that to all our children who've died!"

"Where's Eroth's mercy?" mocked a one-legged man, leaning heavily on a hand-carved stick. "Where's the King's protection when we need it?"

A hulking human, his beefy hands wrapped about the haft of a woodsman's axe swaggered from the crowd. "Things are worse than ever because of you! All your edicts and demands! What have we to do with the capital? The houses look after their own. They don't give a shit about the likes of us."

"You brought this plague upon us!" snapped a wiry merchant. "You stirred up the spirits of the night and cause them to curse this town!"

The messenger shielded himself with his arms as a rain of rocks clattered around him. He tried to shout down his accusers, but even as he moved to defend himself, the mob closed in. The woodsman drove the haft of his axe into the messengers belly, doubling him over as two townsmen seized their helpless prey.

Arryn cursed under her breath as the wagon suddenly lurched. She leaped to the ground, reaching for the blunt kitchen knife in her belt before her boots began to sink into the mud.

"Let it be!" Shael called to her. "This isn't our business."

Arryn ignored her. Boldly she shoved her way through the mob. Surprised men and women scrambled out of her way, the sight of the knife, not to mention the military authority she exuded, forcing them to give ground. She was beside the oak in a moment, her hand closing about the wool hood of one of the villains, seizing the beleaguered messenger. Savagely, she pulled the peasant away causing him to tumble back into the muddy square.

The other forgot his prey and rushed at Arryn, swinging a punch at this new interloper. It was the sort of move that warded off drunks and started bar fights. Arryn's blade slashed out, catching the idiot across the arm. The man staggered back in shock, eyes wide. She watched him carefully, waiting for any sign that her attacker still wanted to fight.

"Who the hell are you?" he growled looking for support from the nearby woodsman and putting himself closer to the mob.

"Someone who doesn't like to see messengers abused by superstitious rabble," she growled back. It was the wrong thing to say. The insult spread like wildfire through the crowd. Angry murmurs spread from mouth to mouth.

"Stay with me," Arryn whispered to the messenger, now cowering behind her. Slowly, the two backed away. She could hear Shael cursing lividly as some of the mob began converge on the wagon.

"You bravery will not go unnoticed," the messenger told Arryn. "I shall inform Lord Gal-Serrek of your actions. Take me from this place and you will be handsomely rewarded."

Arryn rolled her eyes. She knew enough about the noble families to guess that whoever this poor bastard was, he doubtless lacked the political manoeuvring to make such an offer. In fact, she was fairly sure that he'd been sent on this fools errand purely because his sudden departure from the world would not be missed.

Suddenly, a cry went up from the peasants around the wagon. They scurried away from Shael like a pack of whipped dogs. One of them scurried back to a fattened merchant and held a quick conference with him. In moments both men were calling the mob to calm. Arryn and the messenger could only watch in confusion as the ringleaders marched to the wagon. The merchant knelt in the mud and retrieved the leather box that had tumbled from the back of the wagon where the rummaging townsfolk had left it. He glanced inside and hurriedly closed the case. Deferentially, he strode over and handed it up towards Shael.

"My profound apologies lady," he spoke hesitantly. "We had no idea."

Arryn stared in confusion at the peasant's words but if Shael was surprised the scavenger didn't show it. With a scowl on her face, she reached down and took the box. "Did you expect me to travel all in black?" she challenged. "Yes, tell every village and hamlet in the province that there is plague in this town and see how quick they find a new market for their goods!"

Her words had the desired effect. A new fear spread across the faces of the mob. None had considered that the presence of an illness would cause other communities to shun them. The wisdom and foresight of Shael's discretion impressed them more than anything else.

"Forgive us. We didn't think. We assumed our pleas had fallen on deaf ears. Fifteen have already fallen to the rotting sickness and thirty more are sick," he pleaded. "We had already sent a retainer, every coin we could spare. We thought it had been taken and..." his voice drifted off beneath his embarrassment.

"Well, I'm here now," Shael huffed, reaching into the box and withdrawing the mask. "Whose in charge?"

"Dead. Our bailiff too." A nervous twitch pulled at his face. "I... I guess that means that I am."

"And you are?" She demanded, arching one of her eyebrows in an expectant glower.

"Eiflar," the little man answered. "I'm a copper merchant."

"He's the only man who can read and write," the woodsman claimed, hurrying to make himself known. "But if you need anything done, you ask me." He sketched a quick bow. "Gilian."

Shael favoured the brawny human with a thin smile. "Very well friends, I will need suitable accommodation for my assistant and myself. I assume you have taken steps to sequester the infected?"

Both men nodded feverishly.

"Good. You will see to it that I am established away from the area. I will need somewhere large enough to conduct my examinations and a place to secure my instruments." She gestured to the wagon.

"I will see to it immediately." Eiflar stuttered. "You will have the best we have to offer."

Shael nodded. "I expect nothing less."

"When will you begin?" the human woodsman asked hesitantly.

She shot him an irritated look. "Tomorrow. We have ridden far and the reception we have received has been far from welcoming. We will need time to compose ourselves."

Arryn put a hand on the messenger. "I don't think that you will have anything to fear from these degenerates." She smiled but was surprised when the man pulled away from her.

"Keep your foul hands from me!" he spat at her, recoiling from her grip. "Grave rats!"

"Does this man bother you?"

Arryn looked over her shoulder to see Gilian massaging the haft of his axe longingly. She shook her head and turned back to the messenger. "It won't end well for you to end this one. As pitiful as he is, House Gal-Serrek will exact a greater toll from you if you do. Let him talk. It doesn't mean you have to listen. After all, what have the Gal-Serreks' done to help you?" She started back towards the wagon. "That's why my sister and I are here."

Arryn stretched in the enormous bed, sighing contentedly. The manor was situated away from the town on a rise that overlooked the stretching farmland. It had belonged to a lesser lord who, according Eiflar at least, had not been seen in many years. The rooms were musty and scattered with cobwebs but after many days battling the elements and not a few years of sleeping in gutters, it could have been a palace.

She reached over to the tabouret set beside the bed and wrapped her fingers around goblet of wine. A shaky hand brought the vessel to her lips and managed to pour more wine into her mouth than over the fur blankets. She smacked her lips appreciatively, hurling the depleted cup away with exuberant gusto.

Shael laughed. "Eroth's fangs!" She choked on her own cup. "Did you ever see such a spectacle! The whole town eating out of our hand like were the King himself." She leaned against the post of the bed and pointed a finger at Arryn. "I reckon if I went to their seedy excuse of a tavern tonight, I would have my pick of the lads."

Arryn sat up straighter, a frown forming lopsidedly through the veil of alcohol. "But I thought you hated the physics," she began. "Charlatans, that's what you called them."

Shael waved a hand. "Oh, they are." She caught the disapproving glare making it's way across her sister's face. "Cheer up, you idiot!" she snarled. "Too much marching and discipline has ruined you. I knew you should never have signed up for the war."

Arryn rose unsteadily. "You go too far. Mind your tongue!"

A caustic chuckled answered the threat. "If not for me, you'd be lying in the street with your throat cut open. Just another victim of desperation."

"We were starving! We'd marched all the way from the foothills through hail and fog. The King turned out the King's guard on the petitioners, rode them down." She stumbled and caught the bed post. "He gave us steel instead of bread. We fought in his bloody war and he turned us out to starve!"

"It was the King's duty to keep the city's peace," Shael declared, her tone like a lash. "Not to support rioters. Can you blame him for treating you like traitors?" The sardonic levity drained from her voice. "Of course, I'm a traitor too. Helping a dying soldier, when I should have left her body in the street to be hauled away. But for that failing conscience, I might be attending the capital's great and good as a respected Lady."

"So you decide to play at being chiurgeon?" Arryn hissed. "What was that you told me? That we can't hurt the dead any further?"

Shael shrugged and collapsed into an armchair with puff of dust. "These people are already dead. They just don't know it yet." She kicked the leather box. "There's no cure for the rotting death. Even Eroth can't seem to banish it."

"So you'll charge them handsomely for what?" Arryn slurred, tumbling back onto the bed.

"Everything," Shael replied, a dark smile collecting on her face as she steepled her fingers. "Everything they have to offer. I'm not some vagabond scavenger now, little sister. I am Lady Physic, mistress of life and death."

Arryn felt the sickness of over indulgence roil in her stomach. "How does it feel then? How does it feel to be some damned important,"

Shael removed an unopened bottle from the cabinet beside her. Unable to manipulate the stopper, she smashed the neck against the arm. "Good," she replied simply. "Damned good." She chuckled and took a swig from the bottle and sank back with a happy sigh, watching as her sister staggered from the room in outrage. However much Arryn detested her, she knew her sister would stay by her side. There was a debt of honour there, an obligation that Arryn would never cast aside. When this town had given her all that it could offer, Arryn would still be there to accompany her to the next and the next after that.

As she drifted into an inebriated sleep, she fancied that she heard shutters over the window creak open and the impression of scratchy whispers from somewhere inside the room, but she couldn't make out the sounds. The effort only fatigued her the more and soon she was asleep.

The townsfolk kept their distance the next day as Arryn and Shael marched down the muddy street. Shael had donned the horrific mask from the box, her lean body cloaked in a heavy black cloak she had found at the bottom of a wardrobe and she had felt leant her an air of mystery. It swathed her body, covering her from shoulders to ankles. It's hood covered her short cut hair and had an oily sheen from the droplets of rain water.

Arryn followed close behind, nursing a stubborn headache from the night before. She clutched the leather box, reticent about aiding her sister in this cruel deception. Military conditioning prevented her from quite being able to keep the distaste from her face.

"Cheer up," Shael insisted, her voice muffled by the mask. "We'll visit a few of the sick and mutter a bit of impressive sounding dogma, play up a few of their superstitions and head back. Just remember not to touch anything."

"Eroth have mercy!" Arryn groaned.

Shael stopped, turning to stare at her sister and even with her face obscured, Arryn was confident there was sneer behind that mask. "Why shouldn't she? She ought to be a little more concerned about her own children at least."

They proceeded down the street. Turning down a narrow lane, there was a distinct change of atmosphere. An air not of squalor but decay. Here the sunken huts and leaning buildings bar chalk marks upon their doors. Moths. As they continued their promenade, they saw a pair of men hauling a body from one of the houses, employing meat hooks to speed their labour. Unceremoniously, they dumped the body into the back of a cart.

Shael watched the corpse-cart slowly creep down the lane. "Disgusting," she whispered. "And you think that we are bad, sister?"

"They'll be off to soak themselves in vinegar next," Arryn muttered. "It's supposed to fend off the illness."

Shael contorted her face behind the mask. She'd seen brutality her entire life, but there was something chilling about the way peasants treated their dead neighbours.

"I dare say before their shrine-matron died, the bodies were treated with a bit more formality." Arryn observed. "Of course, when she died it probably diminished everyone's appeal for pomp and ceremony." She watched her sister's masked face turn and focus on one of the few solid looking structures.

"Here we are," Shael announced. "Let's see if we can do something to help this unfortunate soul." She rapped on the door with the back of her hand.

After a few moments, the door opened to the face of a young girl, her elegant Drau features still pretty despite the pallor of her skin. By the quality of her clothes it was clear that she was no mere domestic but someone of the household. She drew back in alarm at the masked visage of Shael at the door. However ghoulish the presence was however, she recognised the look of help when she saw it.

"Please, come inside." She murmured. "Thank young for coming at last."

Shael and Arryn slipped across the threshold. "Am I to understand that your family is of some import in this community."

The girl lowered her eyes. "You're kind to suggest it, but my father wasn't really important at all... until... until..." Tears began to well up from her eyes.

"We understand," Arryn said, stopping herself short of reaching out to comfort the upset child. "The sickness has spared neither great nor small. Eroth willing, we might yet spare your father."

Shael nodded and gestured into the house. "If you would take us to your father."

A flash of hope stirred in the girl's eyes and stabbed at Arryn's heart like a dagger. She grabbed Shael by the shoulder, whispering urgently into her ear.

"Leave?" her sister scoffed. "And disappoint this poor child? Now which of us is being cruel?"

Shael let her sister stew beneath the weight of that question while she turned and followed the young Drau down a clay walled hallway to a small chamber at the rear of the house. The room was dark, heavy cloth had been hung in front of the only window, blocking out the meagre light of day. She snapped her fingers, waiting impatiently for Arryn to enter the room and hand her the small leather case. From this, she removed a bloated toad she had caught in front of the manor not an hour ago. Setting the creature on the floor, she gestured to the girl loitering terrified in the doorway. "We must rebalance your father's humours. Tie this creature to the worst of your father's sores. It will draw out the worst of the illness's toxins." She nodded at the window perceiving the slight draft. "You must ensure that you prevent any malign spirits from entering the house. Place a cloth of vinegar beneath every door in this house and on every windowsill. The purifying scent will stave away such predatory wraiths."

The girl's mouth opened to vomit a stream of gratitude. She moved to hug her saviour but Shael leaped back.

"Remove your bodice," she ordered, hearing a sullen growl from her sister which she ignored. She had no ill thought towards the child.

Timidly the girl pulled the drawstring revealing the swollen red lumps that stood exposed. "Please," she begged. "Please don't tell anyone! There is an old woman who brings us food. If she knew I was sick too, she wouldn't come."

"We wont say anything." Arryn jumped in before Shael could reply.

Shael glared at her but slowly nodded. "My associate here will collect our fee."

Arryn maintained a sullen silence as they withdrew from the doomed house and returned to the muddy streets. She gasped for air, releasing a breath she didn't realise she'd been holding. She walked a step behind Shael, her mood growing darker with each footfall. A fraught conscience was not something she could afford since her exile from the city. As her sister would say, if she was to survive in this new world, she was going to have to be ruthless.

"They were both going to die anyway," Shael declared. "At least I gave them some hope in their final hours."

Arryn didn't reply, staring daggers into her sister's back.

"You're upset about the money, aren't you?" Shael continued. "If I hadn't charged her a fee, she wouldn't have believed a thing I said. There's a certain ceremony to these things." She booted a stone from the street with the toe of her foot. "You would prefer if I left everything for Eiflar and the barbarian to squabble over? If you want a pair of vultures, they are right there for you!"

"This isn't right," Arryn muttered. "You took advantage in the most cruel way..."

"Right?" Shael turned and shouted. "Who are you to decide what is right? You stood at the forefront to help your starving friends stand up to what? For that you were left to die in a gutter. Is that right? You need to learn one thing if nothing else little sister. Eroth does not care for little people and even less for their suffering. You take every opportunity that comes your..."

Shael's wisdom was left unspoken, her words trailing into a scream of pain that even the leather mask couldn't muffle. She collapsed forwards, her hands clutching the jagged wound at her side, eyes staring in disbelief at the blood coating her fingers.

Arryn threw down the leather box, letting the contents explode across the street. She reached for a sword she no longer carried out of instinct than anything else. She gazed up and down the street, shielding her eyes against the rain and seeing nothing but an ambling sow. It was devoid of any life. Nearly every door bore a chalk mark sign of infection and if there were any still living in this part of town, they kept themselves behind closed doors.

Save one. One denizen had not stuck to this unspoken rule. As Arryn stalked near to a particularly ramshackle and decaying hut - little more than a lean-to, a shape burst from the decaying roof. A blur of motion and it was upon Shael.

A hand, no, not a hand, a claw, a filthy, verminous brown, claw.

Their attacker could not be human and it certainly could be rejected as any Drau. It was a perversion of life, chittering to itself insanely. It held itself to the posture of any humanoid covered in tattered rags and bits of bone. A wicked blade was rusty with neglect, its edge notched and pitted with age. Blood dripped from its edge, Shael's blood.

Arryn had fought the feral Dwentari of the South and helped slay the wild beasts that had roamed those mountains, but never in her wildest nightmares could she have imagined a creature so repugnant. It hissed through it's sharp fangs at her, a slick black tail lashing with loathsome exuberance.

A pained moan escaped Shael's lips and snapped Arryn from the spell of terror that had gripped her. She owed her life to her sister, what ever crimes and misdeeds stained their souls. Screaming blue murder, she charged the monstrosity.

"The creature snarled at her, whipping its tail into her face with a speed that was nothing short of incredible. Ironically, it was it's very speed that made its blade miss its intended victim. The edge of blade whipped close to Arryn's one good eye before her fist came smashing down on the creatures skull.

Again the amazing speed of the creature was displayed. With a squeal of shock that it had been struck, the hideous creature dropped onto all fours and darted back. Arryn struck out with her foot and felt a burst of pain across her arm as the creature's blade came rushing down. With a grimace she seized the thing's arm, pulling the blade from its grip. Blood was running freely, dripping from her fingertips. She could feel her strength draining from her body. The slinking attacker had sliced an artery. She fought to get back to her feet, her honour demanded nothing less.

Shael was staggering away from the fight. Arryn looked back at her and waved a hand, motioning for her sister to go. "We are even now," she called to her. She reached down and picked up a loose stone roughly the size of her fist, clenching it to brain the creature at the nearest opportunity. "Run," she insisted as the thing hissed and circled like an angry cat. "I won't keep it busy long." A bubble of laughter escaped her lips as she looked at the greenish taint to the skin across her wound. "I am already dead."

Hearing her sister's final request was enough to break Shael's heroic resolve that had so briefly risen. She squashed it like an irritating insect. Standing beside her sister would only see them both die needlessly. Pragmatism drove her into a headlong flight. Behind her she could here the scream of her sister as the creature attacked.

Shael didn't look back, her hand clutched to her own wound.

Every step sent fresh agony through her body. She threw the cape off to one side and tore the mask from her face, sucking in lungfuls of damp air. Clamping both hands to the wound in her side, she could feel fresh blood spurting between her fingers, defying her efforts to pinch the wound shut. Without help she would not last long.

However long she thought she had, Shael found herself cheated. As she limped down another muddy lane, a dark shape bled from the shadows of a haystack, gripping the edge of a serrated blade.

Shael recoiled from the creature, terror pounding in place of her heart. Its face contorted, drinking in the stench of her fear with a peal of merciless laughter.

"What are you!" Shael screamed. "Eroth's mercy! Leave me alone!" she pleaded as the thing crept closer. "I did nothing. I wont speak of this. I promise!"

The creature paused and again its body shook with laughter, tail switching back and forth. A demon, a devil, what foul abyss had spat forth this abomination? Eroth! She was going to die because of a lie, because when she had told the people of this cursed place she could save them, they hadn't been the only ones that had believed her, she realized.

It wasn't long before Shael was a heap of bloody flesh in the mud. The town blamed the messenger, remembering too clearly the man's antagonism. The built a pyre for him. No one even considered the watchful eyes of the skeleton still rustling in the tree.

# Hero's Feast

"Our ways are not your ways, and there shall be to you many strange things."
-Bram Stoker, Dracula

Esken drew the horse to a halt. The sun was low in the sky behind him, casting long shadows through the tortured branches of the trees behind him. Bitter night beckoned. If he'd been alone the half-breed might have been anxious. The deep woods were no place for a young man to be alone. But he wasn't alone. The figure next to him sat astride his own steed, decked in beautiful plate armour that had been polished to a moonlight lustre and a long curved blade decorated in the weaving script of Rhegarsi. A velvet scarf of scarlet spilled over his chest, falling across the emblazoned sigil of three intersecting blades embossed on the metal. His cloak hung from gold rimmed paldrons. He looked like a fey prince from a story book. Indeed, many had compared him to such. Only one man, no, one Drau, could cut such impressive a figure - the King's champion, Aruvian Gal-Serrek, Lord Commander and wielder of the King's justice.

By comparison Esken's titles - herald, errand boy, occasional messenger, if you were counting the polite ones - were pretty unimpressive. Still, to serve beneath such an august Lord, to be placed at the disposal of such a hero, was an honour almost beyond reckoning. Esken was barely sixteen and less than two years service in the service of the Draurhegar. Yet, in the months that he had been placed at Aruvian's disposal he'd already seen things that a man twice his age would only have dreamed of - albeit in his worst nightmares, but nonetheless.

"That's it?" He asked.

"It is." Aruvian's voice was like silk on water. Had he been a woman, Esken would have swooned - there were many ladies who did. Aruvian spoke rarely, but he had leaned that when the lord did, it was wise to take note.

The trees clustered near the road, overhanging as close as they dared as if eager to snatch them the second they dropped their guard.

So had it been for the many days since they had ridden from the battlefront across The Fangs of Eroth. The Shadowglades had been true to their name with each day, filling Esken's dreams with dread.

A few yards ahead, the wood gave way to a clearing, in the failing light it looked little more than a drab and sodden patch of marshy earth, though the manor at it's centre was anything but. An odd place for such an august looking building to be sure. Here, miles from the great capital and a fair distance from the next large town of Sorrowlight. It stood isolated in the bosom of the forest, a sprawling building of stone standing sentinel. The walls surrounding it were high, breached only by a gate of age blackened oak. Elaborate gables decorated the manor's steep roofs rising sharply against the sky. A seal, smoothed by time, of a coronated wolf had been engraved into the doors and gargoyles gripped the eaves with contorted faces. A warm light blossomed from the mullioned windows and a curl of smoke rose from it's many chimneys, evidence that someone was home.

"How should I address him?" Esken asked, feeling once again, extremely ignorant. However, the task of learning the intricacies of courtly terms among is Drau masters, has been a steep learning curve. Many Drau were intolerable of mistakes.

"He is a Marques. Use 'my lord'." Aruvian replied. "Or should you wish, more completely, Marques Sevraen of House Orandur, Vassal Lord of House Trileris, Consul of the Midde-Lands." The Drau smiled. " I suspect the 'Vassal' part will chafe him - so I would stick with 'my lord'."

Esken would once have found such a grand title intimidating, but after serving Aruvian, very little compared.

"I shall ride on and announce you."

Aruvian nodded. His sharp blue eyes, pale as moonlight, glittered.

"You do that."


Their arrival had not been expected - so much was obvious. Yet, despite that, the household put on a good show. Servants, mainly humans preparing to turn in for the night, were dragged from their beds and put to work in the kitchens. The master was roused from his study and arrayed in all his finery and by the time the sun had fully dipped beneath the horizon, a banquet fit for their visitor had been thrown together. Esken found the process immensely amusing. In his brief time serving beneath Lord Gal-Serrek, he had learned that for all his beauty, Aruvian despised this kind of foppish snobbery. Despite this, the combination of irritation and fear on the faces of manor's staff was worth the dangerous trek they had made on its own.

Sevraen's banqueting hall, like all the rooms in the house, was a study of polished excess. The high roof was painted in extravagant if tasteless frescos of popular myths and lit by an oversized candelabra of easily two-hundred candles. The floor was marble, veins of teal and blue flickering at their feet like lightening bolts - to Esken, it looked like the nave of an Erothian shrine. Even the table, carved from a single massive slice of thornwood and over thirty feet in length, had been polished to a mirror sheen, reflecting the light above and sending it scintillating across dozens of crystalline glasses and silverware.

The guests, a dozen of them, were no less opulent. All looked well-bred and beautiful as Drau often did, if a little uncomfortable at the surprise of Aruvian's arrival at their house. Of the two genders present, it was unsurprisingly the ladies who appeared to have recovered best. They were bedecked in gowns of varying hues, draped in pearls and jewellery. Even at short notice they had managed to arrange their hair into tottering grandeur, laced with lines of gold wire and bloodstone studs. The lady of the house, had covered the lines of her extending years admirably, in white powder with berry red lips. They eyed Aruvian with barely contained heat.

By comparison, their male companions shared looks of mutual concern. They were finely turned out, replete with sashes of office, medals, and silk finery. They strutted to their places, muttering quietly, in anticipation as the food arrived.

From his seat on the edge of the chamber, Esken watched the party intently, trying to pick out the ones that Aruvian had told him about. Most of the party were Sevraen's blood, but some were his advisers. Among them Osken Laern, the Marques' personal apothecary, an elderly Drau with a receding hairline and skin that looked like melted candle wax. His fine hair looked wispy even in low light and he minced and preened like a parody of a woman.

At the head of the table sat the Marques himself. Sevraen was powerfully built, though his muscle was beginning to wilt with age. An oversized nose seemed to hook more like a beak and blue veins could be seen just beneath his collar. He held himself like a king though he was easily a head shorter than Aruvian. As he beckoned to the guests to take their seats, his smile showed a row of teeth almost too white to be natural.

"We are honoured," Sevraen began, his vice seeming surprisingly high. "Truly honoured. It is not everyday that this house plays host to such a guest as the King's own champion."

A murmur of appreciation filtered across the table. Aruvian, taking the place of honour at Sevraen's right hand, remained impassive. Esken knew that look. What many mistook for stoicism, was actually an indicator of just how incredibly bored his lord actually was. He had heard it all before. Having exchanged his armour for robes of velvet red lined with black, but to Esken's mind, was still easily the most regal of the room.

"So, let us eat," Sevraen said, "and celebrate this happy..." he faltered, "if surprising occasion."

The guests needed no encouragement. Soon they were shovelling heaps of food onto their plates - wild goose livers, pigeon, stewed hare, pheasant pie, and something dark purple with eggs floating in it, all washed down with generous slugs of rich red wine brought up from the Marques' personal cellar. Esken felt his stomach grumble just looking at it all and realized that he hadn't eaten since the evening of the day before. Like all personal servants, he had been placed behind his master in the event that he would be needed. He wrapped his arms around his stomach uncomfortably and watched as the guests crammed fine food into their mouths. At least his position afforded him an excellent place to listen in to the conversation.

"So, to what do I owe this unexpected pleasure, my lord?" Sevraen asked, munching delicately on a fig dipped in a sweet, golden goo.

"The King has asked me to meet with all his favoured subjects," Aruvian replied. He'd not touched the mounded plate, beyond poking at it with a fluted silver fork.

Sevraen preened at that. Esken allowed himself a private laugh - his lord was a practiced courtier, he knew well how to massage the inflated personalities of nobility, or to put it less delicately, this was not his first rodeo.

"Well, I hope that our efforts for the war front are all up to date?" he laughed nervously, casting a look at his chancellor across the table.

"We are my lord. I can provide the records for inspection." The tin face Drau drawled, giving Aruvian a defiant glare.

"Ah, very good," Sevraen swallowed a large gulp of wine before topping up his glass. "You're not eating, my lord? Is it not to your liking?"

"I am not hungry."

Esken was certain that was a lie. They had not stopped for refreshment and while he had come to expect that, he was fairly sure that his lord was more used to regular meals.

Aruvian's flat refusal cut through the conversation, like a blunt blade. There was a nervous laugh from one of the ladies that died as soon as she realised he wasn't joking.

Esken smiled to himself. This dinner was looking to be most promising. It was only as he cast his eyes longingly along the length of the table that they were caught by the serving girl sitting beside him. She was human, fleshy, and young. His eyes dropped to her chest, appealingly exposed by a low-cut, tight-laced bodice. Quickly he looked back up.

She smiled at him, and her doe-eyes shone in the candlelight.

"Have you eaten?" she mouthed.

"No," he whispered back. "Not since last night."

She pursed her lips prettily. "Come find me after. We'll see what we can do about that."

Esken grinned.

By midnight, the chairs had been kicked back and the guests had tottered drunkenly to their rooms, belching and wiping their mouths of the exorbitant meal. The Marques had taken his leave last of all, having heroically for his size, demolished a four-tier tower of cream and pastry arranged in a pretty good approximation of his own house.

The room stood empty save for Aruvian and Esken. Dull light from the low burning candles cast odd shapes and the table was so slick with grease it seemed to ripple. Esken once again, found himself gazing at the remnants of the meal still arrayed and growing steadily colder, on silver platters. His stomach rumbled. It must have been audible for Aruvian gave him a sideways look.

"Avoid it," he murmured. "It is no food for a warrior."

"Of course, my lord," Essen replied, wishing that his master would depart for his bed so he could attack the resting shin of boar with the same gusto he'd seen his master decapitated a Dwentari ranger.

"You should get some sleep,"

"Yes, my lord."

"Have my armour cleaned."

"Yes, my lord."

Aruvian looked at him curiously. As ever his expression towards him was inscrutable, like trying to read granite albeit the most beautifully carved and flawless piece of granite that had ever rested in the hands of a master artisan.

"Where will you sleep?"

"I have been given quarters above the kitchen," he replied.

"Stay in them tonight and keep your sword beneath your pillow."

Esken felt a knot tighten in his belly and all thoughts of food were suddenly banished from his mind. "Do... do you expect trouble, my lord?"

Aruvian's lips twisted into a cold smile. "I don't drop in on the likes of these for enjoyment," he replied, the contempt barely hidden in his voice. "The King grows concerned about this one."

"Is he behind on his tithes?" asked Esken, remembering the forceful denial of such a fact from the table conversation earlier.

"On the contrary, he is paid in full."

Esken shook his head. Whenever he thought he had mastered the ways of the aristocracy, Aruvian still managed to prove that they were more of a mystery to him.

"I will sleep with one eye open."

Aruvian snorted a laugh but nodded approvingly.

He turned and cast his eye over the table. Esken noticed the same hungry look that had been his own not a minute before.

"Perhaps I will take one of these for later," he spoke quietly to himself, taking a blood-berry pie from the table. Without further comment, he stalked from the room, the door slamming behind him.

Esken held his breath, listening for the heavy footfalls to recede. His ears were not as sharp as that of a Drau but when he could here them no longer and his stomach could take no more, he launched himself at the table. Knowing what was to come, his stomach gurgled with anticipation.

"Careful, " he cautioned himself. "Just a few good bits to keep my strength up."

An hour later, the house was silent. High up in the west tower, the apothecary Osken Laern paced up and down inside his bedchamber. He was still dressed in his finery from the dinner. His bed was turned back but untouched, a large goblet of wine had been drained by his bedside. He had the look of a man who was agitated, it was in the twitch of his fingers. On a simple wooden desk, a curved dagger lay shining unapologetically in the lamp light. It was hard to see, but the hilt was engraved in hard angular text, a far cry from the lace-like subtlety of Rhegarsi.

"Tonight," he spat, though the room appeared empty. "Of all the nights he could have picked..."

There was a knock at the door and Osken froze. Regaining his senses, he took a step in front of the dagger. "Yes?"

The chancellor entered. He looked terrible. His skin, waxy pale before, was now death-mask white and his wisps of hair seemed to have fuzzed with static.

"Osken, you've got to help me!" he groaned through gritted teeth. One hand was clutched to his stomach, the other to his head.

"You're still here?" the apothecary asked, his voice lacking even the trace of empathy.

"What? I'm ill! Surely that is obvious?"

Osken smiled coldly. "Indeed, so it would seem. You should be down in the kitchen with others."

The chancellor crumpled over as his body spasmed. "Eroth's fangs! Can't you give me anything now?" He belched loudly. A thin string of sputum running down his chin.

Osken remained indifferent. "I have no time for this. There is nothing I could give that would help. The fact is that this has been prepared for many months. All for tonight. This night. This one blasted night!"

"For the love of Eroth, Osken!" His stomach shifted and bulged beneath his robes as the sputum became a watery trail of blood. He spasmed in agony. "Help me!"

Osken hunched down beside the tortured chancellor, ignoring the increasingly putrid stench pouring from his skin. "Eroth can't help you now old friend. I'd get down to the kitchen. There others will already be there by now."

The chancellor's eyes rolled in their sockets, turning rheumy and white. Thick hair began to push its way out of his skin, pulsing across his face, spreading with a terrifying speed. His tongue flickered out, black as ink and drooling with saliva. He collapsed on the floor, clenched with pain.

"You will not prevent this," Osken hissed, no longer paying the pitiful wretch any attention. "I don't care who you are. You will not prevent this."

With that, he stalked from the room and padded down the corridor beyond. Behind him the Chancellor was shaking. Caked lumps of blood and bile slopped onto the floor, steaming gently. He remained stricken and twitching on the floor for a few moments more, heaving as his form pulled and stretched.

Then something seemed to change. He lifted his thin face, now elongated and feral. His eyes, or what was left of them ran with thick mucus and shone with a pale amber glow.

"The kitchen!" the thing that had once been the chancellor agreed, the voice was rough like that of an animal. The eyes flashed with a bestial sense of understanding. "The kitchen!"

Then he too was gone, loping across the floor leaving tatters of shed flesh behind him. The door slammed closed and the candle on the desk snuffed out.

No candles burned in the lavish bedroom gifted to Aruvian. The windows were locked tight and the darkness was absolute bar a single shaft of moonlight. Nothing moved. In the depths of the manor, something creaked once before silence resumed.

Slowly, silently, heartbeats passed in the darkness. The door handle of the chamber turned and the door swung inwards on well oiled hinges. Something swathed in darkness drifted into the room with nary more weight than a thought. Quietly, it inched towards the tussled sheets of the bed and a blade raised over the mattress. For a terrible moment it simple hung there, unmoving.

Then, without warning, it plunged downwards, once, twice, three times. Again and again, stabbing into the soft flesh beneath. No noise. The knife was an artful weapon. It had killed many over the years and knew how to find its spot.

Osken adjust the hood of the heavy cloak, shaking. He could feel the warm blood trickle over his fingers. It was done, the feast was safe.

Moving carefully, he went to the table against the far wall. There could be no mistakes. He had to be certain. Swallowing his nausea, he set the candle upon it to burn. It cast a pale glow, illuminating his face from beneath like a horrific skull. The flame shivered in the darkness. The wood floor creaked behind him. He turned, his heart thumping so hard in his chest, he was sure it must audible.

Aruvian smashed his fist hard in the face, causing the apothecary to stagger back.

Osken opened his mouth to yell as the blade of a sword pushed it's way between his rips cutting his words to little more than a gasp. Blood foamed from his open mouth as he slumped to the floor, his expression locked in a final moment of shock and dismay. The dagger rattled as it hit the floor.

"Pathetic," Aruvian muttered.

He walked nudged the dagger with the blooded tip of his blade before wiping it's surface against Osken's cloak. On the bed the blood pie he had secreted from the feast, still leaked.

"So Sevraen does have something to hide then," he muttered to himself. "Let us see what secrets the Marques keeps."

Esken belched contentedly. Perhaps he had over indulged just a little. Still, at least he'd taken the edge off his hunger. He placed the cuirass of Aruvian's armour to one side. The rest of it still lay in the corner of the small loft space he had been granted, mottled with mud and grime from the journey. His master wouldn't need the suit before dawn and he could finish the rest in the grey hours before sunrise if necessary and the girl had been remarkably pretty. Pretty enough to steal a kiss perhaps.

A short sword lay against his bedroll, where Aruvian had warned him to keep it. Perhaps it wouldn't be such a bad idea to take it with him. If the ladies of the court were anything to go by, many women liked the look of an armed man. He wasn't convinced that anything would come of the night worth worrying about, but perhaps it would impress the serving girl - what was her name? He'd need to remember before he found her. From his experience in Aruvian's service, women - even those as lowly as a serving girl, liked to have the little things observed and remembering a name wasn't so much of an ask now was it?

Leanne? Sora? Shanella?

He shook his head. Hopefully it would come back to him. He grabbed the sword, tying the scabbard around his tiny waist, even then it slipped slightly down his hip.

The corridor was blanketed in a preternatural darkness that seemed to suck all light from the air. He held a candle ahead of him with one hand and kept a tight grip on the hilt with the other. The tiny light illuminated only his own steps. There was no sound, no sign of life within the walls of the manor. It was as still as the grave. Now which way were the servant's quarters?

Esken shuffled along, feeling the old wooden floor flex under his light feet. Doors appeared in the gloom, all closed. As if taunting, the house creaked and sighed at his passing. Dimly, he could hear the soft patter of rain outside and the scratching of trees as the night's wind shook their emaciated branches.

At the end of the corridor, a staircase descended. A shimmer of light issued from the bottom of it. He picked up the pace. Perhaps she was waiting for him?

He reached the base of the stairs. Another corridor yawned away from him with fresh doors leading on either side. He reached out and placed a hand tentatively on one of their handles and opened it a fraction. The light reflected from the corpses hanging there. Rabbits, deer, fox, even a bear, their eyes all glinting like mirrors. He pulled back and closed the door with a soft click and pressed on. There was light pouring from the door at the end of the corridor. Strange excitement built inside him at the thought of her rather pleasing shape.

He reached it, making sure that his sword was properly visible. All nice girls liked a man who looked like he could handle himself. Then, with as much gusto as he could manage, he pushed against the solid wood.

The door swung easily and sickly yellow light flooded from the room beyond, sending Esken's shadow skittering for cover. What lay beyond was not Leanne, or Sora, or whatever her name had been. He didn't have time to voice his disappointment. He was too busy screaming.

Aruvian hurried down the corridors, a hooded lantern in hand. The upper levels were abandoned. In fact, the whole place seemed to be deserted. He tried another room and besides the perfectly positioned furniture, found it the same - empty - as all the others. The grand bed was untouched. That in itself was cause for worry. Throwing caution to the wind, he slammed open a dozen more doors, uncaring of who he disturbed or in what state they were in, only to find more empty rooms.

The knot tightened in his stomach and he barged into Esken's loft space, holding the lantern high. He saw his plate armour largely untouched, in the corner of the tiny room. The bedroll was still folded. No sword, and no boy.

"Idiot," he muttered, heading back out. At the end of the corridor, a stair case lead down. Very faintly, he could see yellow light flickering off the top step. He drew his sword, the steel hissed as it left the scabbard. It was a masterful weapon, its spirit could taste battle and it was already thirsting for it.

Aruvian broke into a run, thudding down the stairs and past the empty, gaping doorways. The door at the end glowed like phosphor, misting the looming silhouettes in the room beyond.

"Eroth's fangs!" he cursed, throwing the lantern to one side. He charged through the doorway. Sickly light burned everywhere, a cloying illumination that seemed to writhe in the air around it with a life of its own. Slugs of congealing blood dripped along the lines of mortar and slithered over the stones. The stench of rotting flesh, vomit, and excrement filled the air, making his eyes water.

Once this had been a bakery. There was something that might have been an oven, now lost under a mound of flayed skin and diseased flesh. Flies stalked the air above it. His stomach shuddered at the sight and he was suddenly incredibly thankful he had not partaken of the feast that had been thrown for him.

"Esken!" roared Aruvian, trying to stop the errant fool.

His call was answered, but not by his messenger. The guests from the meal stalked forwards, dragging themselves towards him. Some were still hauling their suits of skin with them but for many what was left of the comely appearance, hung in rags of glistening sinew or from snapping teeth.

"Hail, Lord Aruvian!" The first wolf-like creature mocked, reaching for him with elongated claws. "Welcome to the feast!"

Aruvian ploughed towards it, hacking and heaving his blade into the stinking black fur. The steel sliced through the carrion-flesh like it was parchment, sending gobbets of viscera sailing through the foetid air. There were a dozen of them, just as before. As they loped forwards they dragged at his robes, clawing at them. He batted one aside with the pommel of his sword before plunging the tip deep within the breast of another. He carved them apart like mutton, yet they felt no pain, only clutching at him, scrabbling to sink their fangs into his flesh, trying to latch their slack jaws onto his arms. But, their first transition made them slow and cumbersome.

Aruvian growled, he didn't have time for this. He kicked out at them, shaking one from his boot before kicking the creatures face. It's skull, still soft from the transformation, cracked like eggshell. But, even with two of their number broken upon the ground, they kept coming. Twelve times his blade fell, and twelve times a severed head thumped against the stone, rolling into the growing slurry of body parts.

He pushed aside the twitching torsos and pressed on, racing through the bakery. So this was the horror that Sevraen had been so keen to hide. Why he had shut himself away in his manor and refused the summons of his king.

The further he went the worse it got. A room that might once have been the servants quarters, was coated in a crimson sheen. The servants themselves writhed on the floor, their mouths open in silent terror as their bodies convulsed and spasmed, skin splitting and muscle distending into unnatural shapes. Black fluid pumped across the floor. Some were still lucid enough to claw a hand out towards Aruvian, scrabbling as if suffocating beneath an invisible film. Others seemed to almost be in a state of liquidation as what ever had been done to them, disagreed with their biology.

He killed as many as he could, delivering mercy to those who still breathed and death to those who had passed beyond the natural. A thin scream broke out further ahead. He was coming to the heart of it, he could feel it.

The next room was vast and boiling hot. Massive copper kettles and iron cauldrons simmered and steamed with what manner of foulness, Aruvian did not care to explore. Lumps of too human looking gristle lay scattered across the gore soaked floor. Only the spiders, held aloft on their silken webs, seemed to be at ease with the degrading situation. Everything was in motion in a vile parody of a working kitchen.

"Welcome, honoured guest!"

At the centre of it all was what might once have been Sevraen. His body had grown to obscene proportions, bursting from his fine clothes. Jerky-like flesh hung in clumps against mangy brown fur that sprouted across his chest and back. Where is flesh was still uncovered, it glistened with sweat and a pattern of veins. Fresh muscle twitched and pulled, barely contained within his new form. When he saw Aruvian, he grinned through a raw muzzle, exposing rows of blackened, feral teeth.

"You have picked an auspicious night to visit us!" it drawled, hacking like a cat with a fur ball.

Aruvian said nothing, holding his blade ahead of him in both hands. Eroth's teeth, if this thing wasn't a least as tall as him again! As the beast lunged, he carved into its hackles, exposing dark viscous meat and blood. Sevraen seemed to barely feel it. He opened his swollen jaws and launched at the King's Champion with tooth and claw, his talons shredding Aruvian's velvet robes.

"You can't spoil this!" raved the Marques, gathering itself for another strike. "We've only just got started!"

Fingers too long to be sensible, each tipped with a vicious claw, slashed out. Aruvian felt a sharp pain as they slammed into his chest, sheering the cloth and burrowing into his skin. The strength of the blow was nothing short of staggering. He grunted, feeling the weight of the beast pulling him down.

With a massive effort, Aruvian wrenched himself free of the horror and whirled his blade around in a back-handed arc. The creature pulled back but not fast enough to avoid the precious steel tear across its throat. It screamed and staggered, gasping as brackish blood jettisoned from the wound. Aruvian did not wait for the beast to recuperate. Leaping onto its shoulders he hacked against the creature's neck again and again, sawing through skin, sinew, and muscle. With each strike the wound in his chest pulled, dotting the matted fur with his own blood. At last, with a sickening crack, Sevraen's canine head flopped from its shoulders. For a few scant moments the body continued to writhe and claw before its death throws could catch up with it.

Aruvian struggled free of the beast, wiping the blood from his eyes and face with the sleeve of his robe. A flicker of movement, shifted at the corner of his eye and he swung the blade outwards, panting with exertion.

He turned it aside not a moment too soon. It was Esken.

The mongrel looked ready to die of terror. His face was as pale as bone dust and tears of horror ran down his cheeks.

"What was that?" he squeaked, eyes staring.

Aruvian clamped a hand on his shoulder, holding the boy firmly in place.

"Strength," he commanded. "Go - the way is clear. Take a horse and ride for Sorrowlight. Summon help. At dawn you will find me by the gates."

"You are not coming?"

Aruvian shook his head, once white-gold hair clotted with viscera.

"I have only killed the diners," he growled. "I have yet to find the cook."

The warren of cellars beneath the manor was labyrinthine. A thick haze seemed to pour from the walls. It was like wading through heavy fog. Aruvian went carefully, feeling the slick floor suck at his boots. Wine cellars, salting meats, grain stores, he passed each with nary a word, save perhaps a curse each time a fly dared cross his path.

At the back of the cellars the foundation wall had been burrowed out and edged with timber frames. The room beyond was small, maybe twenty feet square with a ceiling low enough he had to stoop. Jars and earthenware pots were filled with red ooze. Stone niches were overflowing with old wax, the lit candles unable to collectively cast enough light to fully reveal what lay at the centre.

"You are not who I expected," came a woman's voice.

Aruvian paused squinting into the darkness.

"Where is the boy? His flesh was ripe for feeding."

In the centre of the room squatted a horribly deformed woman. She was surrounded by rolls of parchment. each covered in endless lists of ingredients. Her thick lips wept a constant stream of viscous brown liquid. She was dressed in what had once been a tight-laced corset, but the fabric had burst and her distended body flopped across it. Pale flabs of wasted muscle and skin mottled with black. Angry red lines rimmed her eyes, which squinted tight against some raging infection. Boils jostled for prominence against her warts, and a pimpled rash collected in patches around her neck. Her exposed thighs looked more like rotten sides of pork and as for her eyes themselves, they were bloodshot red.

"He's gone," Aruvian replied, doing his best not to vomit, "and I am not so easily wooed."

The woman laughed, a thick glutinous sound as thin bile cascaded down her chin. "A shame," she gurgled. "I don't think you've had many women in your life. That's not what they say about your brother, now there's a man I could cook for!"

Aruvian gritted his teeth. "What are you?"

"Oh, just a kitchen girl. I get around. When they brought me here, the reception was terrible. Now, as you can see, it is much improved." She frowned. "This was to be our party night. I think you've rather spoiled it. How did you know?"

"I didn't," Aruvian replied, preparing to strike. "But, the King has good instincts and The Dragon has been scenting you for months."

He charged towards her, swinging the sword in a glittering arc. The monstrous witch opened her jaws. They stretched far beyond the tolerance of mortal tendons. Rows of needle-teeth glimmered, licked by a red tongue covered in suckers. Her fingers reached up to block the swipe, nails long and curled.

Aruvian moved quickly, drawing on every ounce of his peerless bladesmanship. The fingernails flashed past him as he weaved past her defences cutting a chunk of blubber from an extended forearm with a precise, perfectly aimed strike.

Her neck shot out, extending like a viper. Her teeth snapping as she went for his jugular. Pulling back, her teeth snapped down into his shoulder. He yelled in pain as she tore away, spitting out the cloth in disgust. Then he was on her again, jabbing at her pendulous torso, trying to find the opening he needed.

They swung and parried, teeth and nails against the flickering purity of tempered steel. The blade bit deep, throwing up a fountain of sticky matter. The woman struck back, raking her fingernails his chest and tearing at the wound he had already taken.

He roared in pain, spittle flying from his mouth and tore away from her, blood soaking into his robes. The neck snapped out again, aiming for his eyes, He back stepped at the last moment, slipping in a puddle of blood at his feet and dropping to one hand.

She shrieked with joy and launched herself at him.

Aruvian's thought screamed at him to scrabble away, anything to avoid being enveloped in that horrific tide of diseased flesh. But, instinct could be trumped by experience and he had his opening.

As fast as thought, he lunged forward under the shadow of the looming horror, thrusting his blade upwards and grasping the hilt in both hands. There was a sudden flash of realisation in the witch's eyes but her body was already committed to the task, the momentum irresistible. The steel passed through her neck, driving deep into the morass of tubes, arteries, and veins that swelled beneath, until it exploded out the other side.

She screamed, teeth still snapping at his face, flailing as the blade bite deep

This time there was no retreat. Aruvian kept his face near hers. He didn't smile, but a dark look of triumph lit within his eyes. With a tug he twisted the blade in his grip, feeling the razored edge do its work.

"Dinner is over," he whispered.

Dawn broke, grey and bleak. His body ached, his chest throbbed painfully. Aruvian pushed the great doors of the manor open, letting the heavy air of the dank forest in. It was thick with mulch, but compared to the filth he had just waded through, it might as well have been a mountain breeze. He limped out, clasping his bleeding chest with one hand. The malign force that had lingered in this place, had been purged. All were dead. The only thing that remained was to burn the place to the ground, and there were others who would see to that. Once again, he had done his duty. The King's justice had been dispensed and the task complete. Almost, there was as always, the matter of paperwork.

Just beyond the gates, a lone figure shivered, hunched over a horse and clutching at the reigns as if expecting the creature to bolt at any second. Aruvian went over to him. Esken didn't seem to hear him approach. His eyes were glassy and his teeth were worrying his lower lip.

"Did you find anyone?" Aruvian asked, trying to keep his voice gentle though it didn't come naturally.

Esken's voice shook when he spoke. He looked terrible and had every right to. No mortal creature, no living man should have had to witness such things.

"The town is mustering. I found a boy. They will bring a matron of Eroth with them."

Aruvian nodded with a wince. "Well done boy."

He looked down at his blade, still naked in his hand. Blood and bone chips had lodged in the patterned engravings. It would take forever to clean. He looked back at Esken. The boy had torn open his own lip and blood was beginning to slide down his chin. It was a pity. The half-born was young and promising. His appetites were hot, and he must have been starving. There were so many excuses, even though he'd warned him not to eat the food. The final blow was the worst of all. Aruvian had liked him.

Esken gasped and fell from the horse as the blade slid into his chest as if he were made of butter. He looked up, his eyes imploring. "Is it over?" he asked pitifully, the tears he'd shed, still glistening on his cheeks.

Aruvian raised the blade again, aiming carefully. It would at least be quick.

"Yes, boy," he replied and was surprised to find his voice heavy with grief. "Yes, it is."

"Years of love have been forgot, in the hatred of a minute."
-Edgar Allen Poe,
The Complete Stories and Poems

# *Mud Men*

"You must suffer me to go my dark way."

-Robert Louis Stevenson,
The Strange Case of Dr. Jekyll & Mr. Hyde

Calith looked to the sky, hoping to glimpse a sliver of sunlight amid the bulging purple clouds, but the storm had strangled all light from the heavens.

"When do you think the next patrol will come to relieve us?" Hearon asked, his voice cracked with exhaustion.

How was he to answer that? This was the eighth day that Calith had sat in this muddy wallow. Hearon was young, barely a man, he'd been brought up from the reserves. It was barely his first day.

He pressed a smile to his lips and patted Hearon on the back. "Don't worry, they'll come for us soon," Calith replied. "We'll hole up here for a bit longer." He hoped he sounded convincing. *Yes, we will hold until the relief comes or we die in the mud*, his mind scolded. He closed his eyes and offered a silent plea to Eroth.

A gentle snow that wouldn't lay, fluttered onto his face. Calith grimaced. "I hate snow," he muttered, pulling the fraying, woollen cloak around him. It didn't make much difference.

"That's what you're thinking right now? How much you dislike snow?!" Hearon looked at him surprised. His segmented leather armour, standard issue, was spattered in yellow-brown sludge. Mud caked his legs almost to the knee and dirt lined his pointed features. He wasn't the brightest, but he had quick reflexes and sharp eyes.

"I hate a lot of things," Calith went on, shivering as the cold wind caught him. "Mud, mountains, the Dwentari, but I think I hate snow most of all." He looked across the devastated terrain surrounding them. What had once been a grassy plain, picturesque even with The Fangs of Eroth rising before them, was now a shattered and bleak graveyard of churned mud and standing spears. Briar's snaked across the ground, rising in barbed hedges but the rest of the field was naked earth.

"I hate being away from the city," Hearon chimed in, looking sadly behind him across the distance. "I hate commander Kryne and all his tattle-tales sneaking up behind everyone, listening for any excuse to do the only thing that makes them smile." He looked at Calith and drew his thumb across his throat. "I hate the mud men for bringing their stinking war to our doorstep and I hate the useless noble bastards who sent me here with barely enough supplies to defend myself."

He should have stopped there, but after just one night, his nerves were in tatters. By day heavy fog blanketed the old battle field and by night the sounds and smell of smoke from the Dwentari camp assaulted the senses. Sleep, rest, simply resting the eyelids, was unthinkable because at any moment the bloody Dwentari might decide to break the line without warning - and they would, eventually, a handful of barely manned Drau outposts would not stop them.

"And I hate every stupid officer and idiotic captain deployed to this line. We'll be lucky to get back to our homes with all our limbs intact." Hearon looked wide-eyed at Calith. "Do you even know what they do to those they find? They..."

"I'll get some grog," Calith mumbled. *Eroth's fangs, he hated Grog!* The human stuff smelled like shit and tasted worse. He rummaged in the sack by his side, it was almost rotted through, and pulled out a leather skin that sloshed lazily. He cursed, the contents had partly frozen. He handed it over and it was snatched from his hand.

He looked at Hearon's unlined face. He was so young. Not too long ago, he'd been someone's beautiful boy. The last unfortunate soul to accompany Calith in this gods-forsaken mud pit, had been less tidy. A human mercenary. He'd died begging for death when a Dwentari blade had almost hacked him in two but failed to complete the job enough to grant the barbarian a clean demise. Calith felt his left eye twitch at the memory.

"Do you think we could find enough wood to light a fire?" Hearon asked, emptying the skin with a grimace.

"Not unless you want to bring every mud man within a hundred miles down on you?" Calith looked out across the field as if expecting the enemy to descend upon them at their mere mention.

Across the field, the Drau had dug shallow fox-holes in an attempt to hide their forward line. Calith had helped dig this one. There was an art to it. If they dug them too deep, the mud walls would slowly creep. He'd heard more than a few tales of them falling on sleeping soldiers and smothering them. When morning came, such as it was, there would be no trace of man or hole, just a shallow depression to mark their grave. The thought of mud oozing over him gave Calith waking nightmares. He'd survived in a half-awake state ever since but still found himself shaking with fright, certain that the cold embrace of the earth was closing over his face.

"Blood of Eroth, what was that?" Hearon pointed off to the left.

Calith drew his blade and whipped around for a better look. He moved so fast he almost slid over. Heart hammering in his mouth, he gazed across the rolling plain, turned mud forming small waves like freshly dug graves. The ice in the air clawed at his eyes, blurring them with his own tears and he realised he was panting. *Were they coming? Were they finally coming?* If he couldn't spot them, they would be on them in a heartbeat...

The sound of Hearon chuckling made him snap around. The boy was pointing over at him, doubled up with mirth.

Calith felt the blood pound in his hears. The irresponsible skin sack had just endangered them all.

"You accursed son of a..."

"What's going on?"

The lieutenant stood directly behind them, squatting as he lowered himself over the lip.

*Damn him, sneaking up on them like that,* Calith thought privately. The temptation to denounce the foolish boy was strong. His joke had been dangerous. He needed to be taught a lesson. But one look at the fear in Hearon's face as he watched their superior, rang the rage from him.

"We were just having a little laugh," he muttered. His voice came out small.

"A little laugh?" The lieutenant looked at each of them with hard, accusing eyes. His voice barely contained the disapproving note. Calith looked at the curved, silver knife sheathed at the Drau's waist and found himself wondering just how many unfortunate accidents that blade had performed. He swallowed, determined not to become another one on that tally.

"How are you holding up?" the lieutenant asked, his voice suddenly, inexplicably gentle. A look that might have been mistaken for kindness, lurked in his eyes.

Calith flinched, he'd seen that look before and knew it to be a trap. He contented himself to say nothing while the newcomer sized up Hearon like a viper would a mouse.

"How are you finding Master Calith, Hearon? May I call you Hearon?" The lieutenant pressed.

Hearon mumbled something inaudible.

"I'm sorry?"

"Of course you can call me Hearon, sir."

The lieutenant nodded. "We're all a family here Hearon, it's important that we look out for each other. Any weakness could mean the deaths of hundreds." His words were slow, like oil over water. He smiled like he was trying to seduce a pretty lady. "If someone is weak. If they are showing signs of fatigue, they could get us killed."

*Eroth damn it, the bastard was looking for any excuse!*

"Do you know anyone who might be exhibiting those thing?" The Lieutenant pressed. "Do you know of anyone who might condemn us all to such a horrific death?"

Hearon looked at the ground and shook his head.

"It's all right. Everyone misses their families. We all want to go home. You want to go home, don't you Hearon?"

*Don't reply. Don't say anything,* Calith thought, wishing his words into the boy's head.

"Of course I do!" Hearon started. "My mother has no one else but me! Whose going to look after her if I don't came back?"

The lieutenant nodded, the corners of his mouth twitching to a dangerous smile. "Of course, of course." His voice was so soft that Calith had to strain to hear it. "And just one little mistake, just a little bit of fun, could make that impossible for everyone. The Dwentari could rage down on us from their camps like an avalanche and we would loose the plains. No one would return home. You do realise how serious that is, don't you Hearon?"

Hearon swallowed, his face so pale that Calith thought he'd died of terror. The older Drau knew how this one liked to deal with those they saw as weak. What could he do? He didn't want to die for the idiot. More importantly, he didn't want their blood to soak the bottom of the hole simply because the bully was bored.

"Yes, sir. We understand. No one here is showing any sign of strain," Calith replied, surprising himself with the volume of his own voice.

The lieutenant clapped Hearon on the back, knocking the air out of him. "Excellent, excellent." He breathed. "I glad to hear it. But, you know who to come to if you have such concerns."

Without reply, the lieutenant turned and left, presumably to harass the next group of unfortunates. They watched his spotlessly clean form, until it disappeared into the mist.

"Next time..." Hearon muttered, scowling. "Next time I'll tell him that he's looking weak."

Calith tried to stifle a laugh at that but his nerves were already frayed and it burst from him like a river until tears slid through the dirt on his face. He laughed until his legs were too weak to support himself and then he collapsed against the mud wall.

Their small amount of camaraderie was shattered by the crump of something smashing into the ground behind them. In seconds their laughter was strangled, vanishing as if it has never been. Calith scrambled across the hole and peered over the ledge, shielding his eyes with his hand as if that would aid him in any way. The mist was thickening now, rising from the sodden earth like the spirits of the dead. To the left a rocky out crop burst from the earth like the vertebrae of some buried titan. To the right the plains extended, empty and desolate as any desert he'd ever heard of. In front of them... he concentrated. Their were voices on the air. Not soft, civilised voices. Course and rough noise that demanded no translation. The Dwentari were coming.

He closed his eyes. He wished he could wake up and find that this was just a horrific nightmare. He was tired, tired of this horror show. Death wasn't unknown to the Draurhegar. In the city, just walking down the wrong street at the wrong time could find you in the gutter with your throat slit. But there was always a reason, always a way to buy or beg your way out of trouble. The Dwentari weren't like that, they didn't care. Old or young, frail or firm, they would come screaming at the line to murder and enslave without thought for their own survival.

They'd swarmed this field fifteen times in the space of just a few months. Calith had seen men hacked apart by their saw-toothed weapons or devoured whole by the beasts that followed them into battle. He remembered the stench of blood mixed with mud, the sharp reek of exposed organs, the stink of terror. His hand shook as a wave of nausea threatened to overwhelm him. Though he had always told himself that it was only a matter of time, only a matter of opportunity, that he was just another corpse in the mud, when the matter came down to it, he still knew fear.

"Are they coming?" Hearon's voice broke through his painful thoughts.

Calith swallowed and looked across the plain, knowing that right now any number of his kin were out there feeling exactly the same.

"You can bet they are," he replied gruffly.

The steady thump of collisions continued. His brow furrowed, the Dwentari were trying something new, something undoubtedly horrible. Would they be able to hold?

"We've broken their attacks dozens of times," he tried to smile.

Hearon smiled back, taking on the comforting lie and nodded. "They can't overwhelm us, we'll see them all dead before they try." He looked at Calith with the familiar half-hopeful, half-disbelieving expression of a child asking if the story was true.

"Tactics." The word burst from Calith's mouth before he could stop it. "We have training and reason. They just swarm like insects." He said it with as much earnest as he could muster as if trying to persuade himself of his own words.

"It seemed to work. Hearon settled, although he continued to scan the plain nervously. To keep him from thinking, Calith made sure that his blade was unsheathed and held at the ready. The pounding crept slowly closer and now he could see the enormous contraptions mounted on the horizon. He swallowed, his expression grim. The thunder of the catapults continued, blasting apart the ground ahead. He wanted them to stop. He wanted to shut out the terrible thunder of them inside his head. When would the cursed Dwentari get there? How would they attack? Despite the lies he'd told Hearon, each assault had been different. Every time, they had massacred the Drau until by some miracle they had been repelled.

"How far away are they?" Hearon yelled above the sound of heavy impacts.

"A better question would be what are they firing at?" Calith replied, scanning for some sign of the advancing Drau army.

Nothing. They were abandoned and alone. Calith hung his head, and preyed that Eroth found him worthy enough to offer her protection. Others had done so - it hadn't saved them. Whatever torments Eroth held for the weak and the damned in her grey realm, it couldn't be worse that this.

Fear turned his gut to jelly. He looked to see if he could make out their lieutenant, but he couldn't see anything but fog and mud. *You could run. Flee, get away from this muddy hell hole.* The thought whispered to him like lover.

If he ran, someone else would have to take his place and they might not be as old as him. Eroth, they might be younger than Hearon. He didn't want more children to die. Not like this at least.

The barrage ended. The silence was almost maddening. All he could hear was his own ringing ears. Bursts of voices were snatched away on the breeze. Mud slithered from the impact tremors into the hole. He watched the stuff pool around his feet to his ankles.

Hearon stared at him, eyes wide and staring. His breath puffing in the air in short gasps. "Is... is that it?" he whispered hopefully.

Calith listened. A dull whine vibrated the air.

Then a shape came running out, the lieutenant, his face a bloody mask below his nose. He screamed, coughing, then stumbling. He lurched sideways and fell forward into the mud, and Calith knew that he wouldn't be getting back up.

The whine intensified.

"Eroth have mercy!" Calith screamed as something hammered into the ground a matter of feet from their hole. A head. Rotting a mutilated, but a Drau head all the same, rolled down the slope into the basin. It cracked like an over-ripe melon and thick green mist oozed from it.

Without thinking his hand went to his face as the horrific rain began to fall around them, each exploding with bone and brain matter on impact. He looked around, the mist was feet from him. Hearon was already yelling, trying to climb out of the pit while his hands tore clumps of mud out of the walls. Calith yelled as one wall looming over them began to slide.

He didn't want to die - not like this!

With two fast strides he was behind Hearon. His hands trembled slightly as he reached up for him, hesitating for just a second before ripping him backwards into the mud and steaming heads.

He reached up grabbing the ledge of the hole with one hand while skewering the mud with his sword arm. The blade was no piton. Mud oozed over it. He let the earth have it, shoving his head above the lip coated in congealing soil.

Hearon looked up at Calith in shock and horror before clapping his arms over his head to protect himself from the next volley - leather bladders filled with the same noxious gases. He grabbed Calith's cloak. The older Drau yelled and the mud wall flopped like a lazy drunk on top of them, burying them to their waists. It was as much as

Calith could do to surf the wave back down into the hole. He kicked Hearon away, wading and swimming as the foetid air sought to engulf them. The boy grabbed his shoulder but his fingers slid away. Blood was flowing from the corners of his mouth and down from his nose.

"You traitor..." Hearon gagged and coughed a welter of clotted matter down the front of Calith's armour. For a moment, his mouth continued to work, but only more blood bubbled from it mixed with something black and tar-like. His eyes stared, huge and terrified for but a moment before they rolled up and he dropped face first into the mud convulsing.

Another belch of ordinance thundered from the enemy lines. The ground vibrated under the many impacts. The hole was falling in on itself on all sides, sucking Calith down into it. He lunged desperately as one portion slopped onto his head. He spat the dirt away and shook it from his eyes. Dragging himself inch by inch to firmer ground before finally rolling out like a newly birthed monster.

He looked back at Hearon's corpse just before the mud cascaded over it, burying all evidence of him. And yet, he lived. He almost laughed madly at that. He lived and Eroth willing, he would continue to do so.

He'd had to kill Hearon. *Eroth below, the boy would never have survived anyway,* he told himself. He'd done the child a service, sent him fast on his way the the Grey Lands. A hero of the Draurhegar no less. Eroth would welcome him with open hands. He staggered away from the flowing mists, clawing at the mud that covered him. The slithering sensation of it over his head and face made his skin crawl.

Calith dared to look back towards the mountains. When would the damned mud men descend on them? When would this terrible anticipation be over?

He felt the cold kiss of steel between his shoulder blades.

"Turn around." The soldier was indistinguishable from any other, slathered in a coating of mud like himself. Reluctantly he did.

"You killed him, you killed one of our own!"

He couldn't make out the features of the Drau's face but he could here the condemnation in his throat. Eroth, someone must have seen. Help had been on the way after all and they had seen him send the boy to his death. Warmth ran down his leg.

The ground shook again and a shadow enveloped them as something large stalked its way through the mud. The shape of it loomed over them, a black silhouette in the fog, accompanied by a ghastly sucking sound that made his toes curl. The shadow grew until it was taller than a horse, taller than perhaps two.

Nearly frozen with horror, Calith only just managed to recover his senses to swipe the creatures reptilian face a moment after it came into view. It shrieked like metal being tortured beyond its strength, but the blade had barely grazed it. Its rattling sound gained more from surprise than pain.

Still it came on. Calith screamed as he tried to back away. The snapping jaws were filled with knife-long teeth and just as sharp. His accuser was not so lucky. The Drau screamed in agony for a split second before he was gone, devoured into the creature's enormous mouth. Around it the bombardment continued, lumps of rock smashed into its bony protrusions, snapping a few, but the gigantic creature didn't even acknowledge their impacts.

A lashing tail, caught Calith across the face and something in his jaw cracked from the impact. He could taste blood in his mouth as he staggered back. It hung uselessly to one side, preventing him from uttering anything intelligible. He fell, dropping into the mud, crawling and crying. He could feel the creatures hot breath against his back and he issued a half-formed scream.

The noise of it was cut short when the beast mouth closed over his legs and punched into the meat of his thigh. It tossed him into the air like a rag doll before snapping him from the air. Calith punched and wailed, unable to voice the pain as the creatures massive tongue began to pull and it's teeth started chewing. Black spots settled in his vision and smothered his sight turning everything first to darkness and then to white.

The creature clenched its jaw with a bone-grinding snap. Calith watched it swallowed something as he was smashed into the ground. A barbaric yell and rattle of chain, forced the creature onwards. After a little time the sound of battle ebbed, the confusion and chaos moved away and Calith's body, or at least his torso, was left alone in the quiet. Slowly, it sank into the mud and was lost.

# GLOSSARY OF TERMS AND NAMES

**Agrellon** - *An eastern city known for it's training of Watchers.*
**Bone-Men** - *Part dead constructs also known as Harvesters among other names.*
**Bloodstone** - *A precious gem similar to Agate, in crimson red. Native to The Lands of the Draurhegar. Sometimes washed up on beaches.*
**Bloodwood** - *A dangerous flora native to the Lands of the Draurhegar. Sentient, violent, and vampiric.*
**Darktide** - *A castle and surrounding town in the north-east. Castle Darktide is foremost known as a college for arcane students.*
**Dhal-Marrah** - *A noble house of the Drau. Assassins and executioners. Sometimes referred to as The Dragon for their sigil.*
**Draurhegar/ Drau** - *The people whose lands stretch from the Bay of Tears to the Mouth of Malinax.*
**Dwentar/Dwentari** - *The people of the south who come from those lands known as The Dwentar Empire.*
**Eroth** - *A goddess. Patron of the Drau. Also known as The Moth Queen. She resides in the Grey Lands. Commonly used when cursing.*
**Everfall** - *The capital city of the Drau. Twice the size of central London.*
**Fangs of Eroth, The** - *The southern mountain range.*
**Gal-Serrek** - *A noble house of the Drau. Warriors and artificers. Their sigil is three intersecting blades.*
**Grey Lands, The** - *The place Drau believe they will return to after death. Presided over by the Goddess Eroth.*
**Grog** - *An alcoholic beverage that is very cheap and made by humans for sea-bound journeys.*
**Iron Lord, The** - *King and Emperor of the Dwentari.*
**Mouth, The** - *The pinching point where where The Mouth of Malinax coastline meets The Fangs of Eroth.*
**Matron** - *A disciple/ clergy of Eroth. Residing at a shrine or temple of Eroth. Temples are presided over by matrons beneath the auspice of a matron mother.*

**Half-Breed** - *Drau racial slur for someone whose parentage includes only one Drau parent. Also referred to as Mongrels and Half Born.*

**Mongrel** - *See 'Half-Breed'*

**Mud-Men** - *Drau slur for a Dwentari.*

**Orandur** - *A lesser noble house.*

**Physic** - *Abbreviation of 'physician'. Applied specifically to people who are not certified apothecaries. Most are charlatans.*

**Rhegarsi** - *The language and native tongue of the Draurhegar.*

**Silver Fortress, The** - *The centre of power for the Dwentari. Lies in their capital city of Kherdrom.*

**Sithaxi** - *A war beast of the Dwentari army. Ridden in infancy by a single occupant but can grow to twenty feet in length to carry more riders or as a beast of burden. Carnivore.*

**Sorrowlight** - *A large town and common stopping point for merchants travelling north.*

**Trileris** - *A noble house of the Drau. Their sigil is three coins.*

**Urghuls** - *Cannibals. Usually nocturnal or subterranean.*

**Watcher** - *A warden of the wild. Usually solitary hunters that are designated with the eradication of threats that affect the natural balance.*

**Witch-King** - *Dwentari slur for the Drau monarch.*


*A Note on Name Pronunciation:*

*Drau and Dwentari names have some unifying features. Drau names where the letters 'a' and 'e' are conjoined e.g: 'ae' or 'ea', the letters are pronounced uniquely. For example the Drau name 'Aerith' is pronounced 'A-e-rith' and not 'Air-rith' and 'Hearon' is pronounced 'He-a-ron' and not 'H-air-ron'.*

*Dwentari and Drau names that feature an 'h' after the first e.g: Zhegra. In each case the 'h' is silent unless it is preceded by the letter 'c'.*

# DRAU BLOOD

**E S STEPHENS**

*A Cerberus & Cerberex Novel*

# DRAU
# BLOOD

*Sample Excerpt*

Whenever and wherever the rich and the powerful descended in numbers, the dregs of society naturally followed in their wake, eager to snap up the scraps. Ever had it been and Cerberus was well aware of it.

Dusk had fallen and Cerberus was had spent the better half of the day either sleeping or examining the precious few schematic sketches the house library had in its possession. Now, the streets around the palace gate were thick with traffic and bathed in a deep magenta half-light. Cerberus fluttered from one group of people to the next like a ghost, analysing the Great Gate from all directions. Carriages bearing the colours of the houses Trileris, Estealia, and of course, Gal-Serrek, rumbled passed, ignoring the mob and rabble. Cerberus watched each pause at the gate offering a parchment to a plate armoured captain before the heavy guard presence of the gate itself, moved aside, allowing the carriage access. He pulled his hood further over his face as he inched closer. As the final carriage entered the gates the crowds surged forwards. For the most part the guards simply pushed them back, some more forcefully than others; but there were those who filtered through. Among the rabble Cerberus could make out artists, performers, escorts, and more. Peering over the shoulder of a rotund sell-sword wearing no particular markings of his loyalty, he watched a female Drau in sumptuous purple silks approach with an entourage of four or five ladies all elven from the northern plains, past The Range Quadrata.

Cerberus was familiar with her, if only briefly. Her name if he recalled correctly, was Belladonna. A half-breed of great repute in the city's night-life. Her establishment, The Black Orchid, was a hot spot for young lordlings with coin to burn and a taste for the exotic. He noticed the two ladies in her group particularly - moon-elves. Their tall frame, pearl-white, almost translucent skin, and elongated fingers made them impossible to miss. So, someone was paying handsomely for the best entertainment in the city - whoever this cousin of the King's was he had to be a Drau in great favour. Belladonna smiled at the captain while her ladies chatted and laughed coquettishly with the other guards. Cerberus watched a purse exchange between them and smiled - *or not.*

Suddenly, Cerberus's view was blocked. He craned his neck as he felt the heavy tremor of the gate open slightly. Bright streamers and a cacophony of different musics assaulted his eyes and ears. The procession of ten or so strong, wound its way towards the gates. Each was masked and lead by a male Drau of aged years in a long coat of cerulean blue and gold that looked too elaborate for even a royal soiree. Cerberus mingled into the middle of the group as they passed, pulling his cloak about him in the hope that their showing off might avert the guards' eyes as he moved with them. They at least, wouldn't notice his presence given the heavy stench of Amberleaf exuding from them.

Their leader spread his arms wide as if to embrace the captain as he approached. Each finger was ringed in gems most of which Cerberus noted, were fakes. "Good evening, most excellent men of the guard." His voice was drawling and ever so slightly slurred.

"If you have no invite, you have no entry here. Move on." The captain slowly moved his hand, making a point to rest it on the blade at his side.

"Behold the bounty of Khathar and join the revelry." The leader continued, undaunted by the captain's intimate threat."

Cerberus twitched slightly at the mention of Khathar. That at least explained the Amber-leaf. Most considered Khathar a false god. But, his edicts of pleasure and celebration had been steadily gaining ground among the youth of the city much to the chagrin of the more orthodox Cult of Eroth.

"Every joyous action, every intimate celebration is pleasing to the Master of Pleasures and where his worship is made, the children of Khathar may enter!"

Cerberus hunched as much as he could while the captain looked over the motley crew of performers. "Actors then. So tell me fool, what role does that one play?" The captain's head nodded in Cerberus's direction and he felt a sudden wave of panic wash over him.

The leader turned to look. A brief glimmer of surprise brushed his painted features before he turned back. "Why he plays the part of sorrow of course. For only with sorrow can we experience true joy." Cerberus did his best to stifle the laugh he felt deep in his gut, Fool he may be, but this one had a silver tongue and a sharp mind.

For a long time the captain seemed to appraise the group before turning and motioning to the guards still at the gate. "The King is a great lover of the arts, let's see just how good you are."

The rumble of the gates vibrated through the stone slabs beneath his feet. Cerberus felt the press of the performers around him shift and moved with them. As they passed underneath, the leader hung back before stepping into stride with him and wrapping an arm around his shoulders. Cerberus instinctively dipped his head lower. "Welcome little brother. I must apologise that I did not see you before but fear not, those who wish to be born anew will never be turned away from Kathar's embrace." His arms were incredibly strong for his frame. He leant down and whispered into Cerberus's ear. "Oh, I know you wished only to see how the great and powerful take their time, but even this small step to witness joy unbound, is a step nonetheless." Cerberus wasn't sure if the old coot was still playing the part or if he actually believed his own act. Whichever it was, he had little time to consider it before the group were ushered into the palace itself.

Cerberus was not new to the palace and while others around him looked aghast at the extravagance, Cerberus could vaguely remember a time when the house of Dhal-Marrah would attend the royal court and Drau courtiers would move from their path at the mere sight of them. In those days, the ceilings and walkways were hung with the banners and colours of every house. Now the stairs, landings, and halls were draped in the bold red and black of house Gal-Serrek, such that the royal house of Lotheri was but a side note. Dozens of servants in black, washed around them. Each busy with the sudden surprise of so many guests. An ancient Drau, his back hunched with age, greeted the entertainers with a curt nod. Cerberus did not catch the words that were exchanged to those few selected for the evenings entertainment in the clamour of the great hall. After a moment or so the group was on the move again, laughing and dancing with each other as they jostled forwards.

Cerberus was content to let them pass as they were lead through a number of small hallways designed to grant the numberless servants and cohorts of guard access through the palace without disturbing their superiors. Eventually, he found himself brought out to a walled garden of exotic blooming flowers that exuded a powerful bio-luminescence and marble pools of crystal water in which swam tiny jellyfish. Floating lanterns of coloured parchment levitated above, held from floating away by some arcane means. The air was heavy with the scent of lavender and violet.

Cerberus hung back and merged into the sea of grey, browns, and blacks of a battalion of house servants en route to see that the needs of the guests were met. He pressed himself against the outside wall of the palace as they dispersed and obscured himself behind a planter. Looking across at the guests, he was suddenly very aware of how much his dark clothes would stand out against the silks and velvets of the lords and ladies in attendance. The flicker of a fan and the brush of skin brought him back to the here and now as he felt a presence of another at his side.

"Quite the party, is it not?" The female voice was accented and decadent.

Cerberus nodded.

"Though I feel it is rather poor taste. I hear the King's cousin is a scholar of the arcane, so he is unlikely to appreciate the quality of the effort."

Cerberus glanced to one side and noted the purple silk, the grey yet tinged with brown skin, the full lips painted an earthy red. and the thin scar that ran from the back of the ear all the way down her neck. He gave a slight smile. "Though there are some of us here that can appreciate it at least."

She caught his eye. "Some I think, weren't invited."

Cerberus sighed. "You are as astute as ever Madam."

"Ah, there I was thinking you were ignoring me... my Lord Dhal-Marrah." She whispered the last bit enticingly. "Though I must say, I am surprised to see you join the party. Perhaps you have a thing for one of the ladies?"

Cerberus sighed. "Alas, I am not here to cause mischief or mayhem."

Belladonna pouted. "And now I am sad. I rather enjoyed your mischief the last time we met." She flicked her fan, doing a poor job of hiding her grin.

Cerberus tilted his head. "You're all work I see."

"Well, a lady must make ends meet." She sniffed. "Besides, I don't hear you complaining."

A blast of silver trumpets disrupted the casual atmosphere. "Their royal highnesses, King Aelnar Gal-Serrek and Queen Lida Lotheri." The guests turned and Cerberus pressed himself against the wall.

"Place your arm around my waist and no one will question you. They will think you simply my bodyguard." Belladonna seized his arm and wrapped it around her before forcing him into a bow as the King and Queen entered the garden followed by a heavily robed individual.

Immediately, every individual fell to one knee. King Aelnar couldn't hide his smirk as he strode with every air of confidence, dressed in a deep crimson robe clearly meant for an individual a good size smaller than he was. He strode ahead, his arms outstretched. The Queen, by comparison, was modestly dressed in lavender. A floor length gown of lace and chiffon without adornment save for the silver filigree circlet of office that accentuated around her ears. Cerberus felt a stab at his ribs and a strong arm force him down further.

"Friends and honoured guests. Not since the day of my binding, have I had occasion to throw such an extravagant soiree but today is one of great celebration. It gives me great joy to finally introduce my own cousin to our esteemed company. Too long has he served in shadow. It is time that he was recognised.

As the King turned away, Cerberus drew out of the bow and glanced at the newcomer.

"Vor'ran." The King clasped both hands heavily on the new individual's shoulders, who winced but remained smiling. "I am pleased to finally bestow upon you the honour you have so long been denied. You have served as my loyal aide and friend for too long without recompense." Cerberus watched with narrowed eyes as the King withdrew a on golden chain upon which hung a medallion emblazoned with a large ruby and hung it about the Drau's neck. The King turned to the party. "Behold Vor'ran of House Gal-Serrek. Lord Adjutant of the King."

The Drau adjusted the medallion, pulling his hand out of the sleeves that had hidden them and setting back the hood that covered his face. His long coat was a vibrant arterial red, arcane glyphs had been picked out in silver thread that seemed to sparkle in the light and all this trimmed in white wolf fur. His skin seemed mid-grey neither dark nor light and his extra-ordinarily round head was completely shaved of hair. Cerberus didn't need any of this to know he had met him before or someone like him. Though time had begun to show the signs of age with a slight wrinkle set perpetually above the eyes, running around to both ears. Here stood the nightmare that had haunted his sleep for a hundred years, made flesh and blood and smiling amiably to any who looked at him. Here stood the bane of Dhal-Marrah. Their fall form grace made possible only by the hands of this Drau and the blood that lay upon them. Dhal-Marrah blood, his father's blood. Cerberus breathed heavily, his body seeming to switch from ice cold to burning hot. The transition made him want to throw back his hood and gasp for air, instead his hand held tight to the rapier he had hidden beneath his cloak, his thumb stroking the engrave 'D' on the pommel. For a moment he was sure that his fingers were glowing red, then his hands, then his eyes began to sting. When he looked up, Vor'ran had mingled with the party and though it felt like seconds, it seemed minutes had passed.

"Are you listening to me?" Belladonna's face creased with annoyance.

"I'm sorry Madam?" Cerberus blinked away the brightness blinding his eyes.

Belladonna glanced under his hood. "Eroth's teeth, have you been touching the Amberleaf?" She scolded and huffed. "Keep your hood up ad your face down then, I don't want you embarrassing me." Cerberus lowered his head and nodded.

"Madam Donna? I don't remember extending an invitation." A skinny individual in a handsome emerald green coat with antique gold brocade, inclined his head. Cerberus knew this Drau also. Malinar was his name or more usually, Lord Trileris.

Belladonna dipped in her skirts just enough to be deemed acceptable. "My Lord Trileris. I simply assumed that in the heat of all the planning, my invite had simply been forgotten." She gave him an evil smile. "Naturally, I couldn't let you simply be hung out to dry after all the work you'd done and a party isn't a party without some entertainment." She brought her head to his ear. "And I am something of a collector of the most exquisite types of entertainment as you have seen for yourself once or twice."

Cerberus watched Malinar's face twitch into a smile. "How very thoughtful." He paused. "You seem to be without refreshment, Madam. Let us see if we can't do something about that." He held out his arm, giving Cerberus a curious look.

Belladonna accepted it, wrapping both her hands around the bicep.

"Oh, don't worry about my man here. It's simply a precaution to ensure that my ladies and I came across town ... unmolested."

"Indeed, perhaps he would like to remove his hood and cloak. It is a warm enough evening, surely." He inclined gently to peer beneath the hood.

Belladonna grasped his chin between thumb and forefinger. "I would not recommend it, my lord. The beast was facially scarred by his previous owner and I insist he keeps himself covered for the sake of decency."

Malinar drew back. "Well, we wouldn't want that now." He smiled, all ease and friendliness. "I believe I offered you a drink? Come, let's see what the royal wine cellar has brought for us and you can tell me about all the city's latest rumours. It's been a while since I could get out and about."

Belladonna smile graciously. "It would be my honour."

The pair moved across the garden. Weaving between the guests, Cerberus followed them while maintaining what he hoped was a reasonable distance. His eyes twitched left and right for any sign of wolf fur trim or a flash of scarlet, but he saw only lords and ladies familiar to court exchanging in polite, well-groomed conversation. Out of the corner of his vision he caught sight of the King and Queen surrounded by a gaggle of over-absorbent lords and ladies out to gain favour and a better seat at court. The King seemed to be well into his cups already. As for the Queen, her face was one of deadpan acceptance. Cerberus gritted his teeth. What did she see in him? His focus was so bent on the commotion the royal couple caused, he did not catch himself before walking directly into Malinar and spilling his goblet down the lord's embroidered doublet.

"What in the..." Malinar looked at him angrily as Cerberus rebounded away. "Madam, if your bodyguard cannot behave properly then maybe you are not welcome at this gathering." He hissed, wiping at the deep red stain.

"A thousand apologies, my lord." Belladonna looked mortified before her face changed to one of anger. "You idiot! Be gone until I call for you."

Cerberus gave a deep bow, allowing his hood to slip lower over his face till he almost couldn't see, and then moved in a roundabout way to the table of refreshments being constantly attended to by a handful of human females. Surreptitiously, he took a goblet and knocked back the contents before replacing it. It was an extremely fine vintage. A little earthy for his liking but he could appreciate it nonetheless and the brief hit of alcohol was a pleasant relief. His hand went back to his rapier. Where was Vor'ran? It was like the Drau had suddenly disappeared or had vacated the party in some way. But, the garden was an internal courtyard, walled on all sides by the palace itself and only a single entrance and exit. He moved quietly from group to group, all the time keeping his wits about him.

A loud laugh from the growing circle of flatterers around the King and Queen made Cerberus look up.

"So that's when I told her - lady, all I need from you is a shot and you on a table with your skirts above your head!" The King belched with laughter echoed a split second later by the rest of the gathering. He turned and pushed an empty goblet into the Queen's hands. "Fetch me another," he ordered before catching himself, "my dear." He turned away from her. "These excellent people seem to be enjoying my little stories immensely."

The Queen stared for a moment at the goblet in her hands. Cerberus edged to a closer group, remaining out of sight. "Tell him to get it himself." He urged her mentally, willing her to turn and throw it in he King's face. He watched as she sighed inwardly and made her way to the table before handing it to an awaiting servant. "How low have you fallen?" He muttered to himself in disgust even as he drew closer, masked by a group entranced by the dancing of a nearby moon-elf.

"I see you pay continuous attention to the King's needs."

Cerberus ducked as Vor'ran seemed to suddenly appear from out of nowhere. The Queen simply looked at him, her face a mask of annoyance at a task she had been caught performing and the irritation at the complete lack of formality Vor'ran afforded to her. "It's rare to see a Drau such as yourself, still able to perform such menial tasks without the need for others." He patted her arm. She stared at the irreverence of the gesture in fury. "I think it shows a level of modesty many of us could learn from."

"Cousin!" The shout came from the ever growing gaggle.

Vor'ran smiled and waved before turning back to the Queen and handing her his own goblet. "Excuse me, my lady, it would appear I have been summoned."

Cerberus watched him meander his way towards the King, before returning his attention back to the Queen.

Her head was bent over, hands placed squarely upon the table. Cerberus inched up a fraction, peering over the groups heads. She seemed to be ever so slightly shaking and judging by the look of concern on the servant's face, not for joy. Was she... weeping?

She brushed a hand over her face and took a couple of deep breaths bringing her bearing straight and looking over the guests. Cerberus ducked. Turning back to the table, she pulled forward two goblets downing the first and discarding it before pulling a third to replace it. Motioning, she held up the empty goblet with a look of distaste, attracting the attention of waiting servants. Cerberus didn't catch the conversation but watched as both humans nodded quickly and immediately left, presumably for some beverage that better fitted the Queen's demands. As they left, she reached down her slight cleavage and withdrew what initially Cerberus thought to be a sliver of glass. Shifting as close as he dared behind a pair lost in the moment with each other and smelling strongly of wine, he realised as she snapped the top away, it was a tiny vial of black liquid; barely enough to coat a knife edge. Deftly, she slipped the contents into one of the goblets and seizing it to her chest, looked up, and breathed nervously...

# NEED MORE...

WWW.ESSTEPHENSAUTHOR.CO.UK/BOOKS

**ABOUT THE AUTHOR:**

Elizabeth S Stephens lives in the riverside town of Kings Lynn on the Norfolk coast of the United Kingdom. She can often be found in a dark corner, writing tales in the Modern Gothic genre or travelling across the country to meet and talk about writing in high schools, colleges, and libraries.
Author of the globally sold Lands of the Draurhegar Series, she has been listed at #1 for The Best of Spring Reading 2020 by Einswire Press, #8 in 20 Must Reads for Fall 2020 cited by CBS, and listed among Authors to Read for National Authors Day (USA). Her flagship series is a wild ride of murder, assassination, and epic fantasy.

Lightning Source UK Ltd.
Milton Keynes UK
UKHW040727050521
383164UK00001B/66

9 781034 896463